THE CRIMINAL'S CRUCIBLE

Previous Works

1-The Criminology Society
(Feb 2, 2022)

2-The Criminology Chronicles
(May 29, 2023)

3-Detective Dark
(Nov 15, 2023)

The Criminal's Crucible

J.L. DUMIRE

J.L. Dumire

Contents

Prologue

To the Criminology Society

It brings me great pleasure to notify you all that I will be returning to Oxford soon. However, as good as that news is, with me comes a modicum of devastating events that I would like your help with. My visit back to the States has fully reminded me of why I spend so much time in Europe. Apologies that upon my triumphant return, I must impose my troubles onto my friends, but I've learned one thing from our recent collective experiences. I can always count on all of you for the greatest or even the least of problems.

Ever inebriated,
James Mondey

Chapter One

Cecil Blackbird, the butler of the home known as Everjust, was making his rounds before luncheon would be served. As always, he was the first one up in the morning. Five o'clock, bright and early, without fail as though he were some sort of wind-up automaton. The tense young man ran his fingers through his raven hair and took a look down at his fob watch.

"Nearly eleven." Mr Blackbird grumbled to himself. "Miss Cyrus?" He called out as he approached the bottom of the stair.

The petite maid obliged her custodial compatriot by poking her head over the edge of the bannister on the second floor.

"Yes, Cecil?" She queried with a chipper tone in her voice. Essie Cyrus had been up since seven o'clock catching up on her work, but all the same her hair was much more relaxed under her maid's cap. Her clothes were immaculate but she seemed to have only brushed her hair and tucked it behind her ears today, leaving her wavy brown locks free to sway.

"Where's Roland? I never saw him at breakfast." Cecil was at attention but despite his unmoving stance, Essie could tell he was perturbed. "In point of fact, I haven't actually *seen* him at all today!"

"He isn't home." Essie's statement clearly upset the uptight man as he snapped the watch shut and she could swear there was a twitch in his eye. Cecil took a deep breath and grunted, attempting to keep from yelling.

"Then where in the hell is he?" Mr Blackbird asked in an uncharacteristically sweet tone that made Essie stifle a snicker.

"He's gone down to the train station to pick up James on his arrival. He told you, but I think you were too busy to listen." Essie chuckled.

"Ugh!" Cecil pocketed his watch. "He should know better than to bother me with triviality while I'm working!"

"I'd hardly refer to bringing Mr Mondey home as '*triviality*'." Essie chuckled as she began descending the stairs.

"Oxford is not *technically* his home, *nor* are the States. He's more of a globe trotter, by definition." The butler stood eye to eye as Essie stopped on the third step to remain at equal height. "I believe there is a colloquialism that goes something like; He is here for a good time, not a long time."

"True, that's James Mondey to a tee." Essie completed her downward scale and took the lead as they both crossed into the dining room on their way to the kitchen.

"However, I believe Mr Wood extended an invitation to James to stay here at Everjust." Essie allowed the swinging door to the kitchen to swing freely, noticing that Cecil was not following her... until he kicked the door open unceremoniously.

"*Absolutely not!*" shouted Cecil. "I'll not have that hedonistic nutter dragging his tarts in and out of here mucking up *my* schedule!"

"To say nothing of draining our stores of liquor and whatnots." Cook chimed in as she continued fixing lunch with an amused smile on her face. "I love the lad, but he's terrible for keeping house around."

"It is for those reasons, exactly, that I highly doubt Mr Mondey will accept the invitation," Essie held up her hands to her two professional friends. "So I believe you can both rest easy."

Cecil seemed to breathe a sigh of relief until the sound of a motorcar pulling up in front of the house drew his attention. He took a glance at his watch and realized that one of the other members of the Criminology Society must have just arrived. Hurriedly, he rushed to the front door to perform his duty and greet their guests. Mr Blackbird adjusted his vest and opened the front door to see Susan Jordain and Andrea Karras, the latter reaching out to open the door. Cecil took notice of the fact that Andrea was reaching for the door handle rather than rapping at the door.

"Not one for knocking, are we?" He arched his eyebrows in an imperious way.

"Oh, don't be such a toff, Cecil." Andrea replied with a smirk as she crossed her arms.

"Andrea, play nice. We're guests when we come here." Susan chided.

"James arrived yet?" The streetwise maid questioned as she removed the small round sunglasses she was wearing from her face. Her eye makeup was rather heavy, but that was hardly astray from Miss Karras's version of normal. She arrived in a black low-cut jacket with red trim and a similarly coloured silk scarf tied 'round her neck, along with some high-rise trousers and a cloche hat adorning her black bobbed hair.

"Not as of yet, but Roland has gone to the train station to wait for his arrival." Cecil guided the ladies into the house. "Now I know that you two must be vexed with keeping up your facade of professionalism, so shall I draw the curtains on the front rooms?" He asked as he took Susan's light blue shawl from her shoulders. Susan was in an equal and opposite outfit to her paramour, as always. The two always looked like an angel and devil arm in arm each time they arrived. Susan wore a fine white blouse with a popped collar and a blue skirt, parted by a wide belt with a silver ring in her midsection.

"No need, Cec," Andrea stated. "It's just a social visit to see Jimmy, after all." The maid cosied up to her friend and employer as the two intertwined their fingers. "'Sides, there's a certain thrill to the risk of playing a dangerous game."

"Don't call me 'Cec'." Cecil shook his head as he hung Susan's shawl.

Essie came trotting into the foyer to also greet their dear friends. The perk in her step was evident as she placed her hands together to hold in her excitement.

"Hello, Susan, Andrea!" She beamed.

"Essie!" Andrea swept Essie into a tight hug. "Been too long, lovey!"

"You were here only last week." Essie chuckled at the absurdity of the statement.

"That *is* too long." Andrea insisted. Susan nodded in agreement as she too hugged Essie but in a far more gentle fashion.

"Has anyone figured out what it is that James wants our aid in?" Susan inquired.

"Haven't the foggiest. Go on and take your seats and we'll begin pulling some lunch in." Cecil shooed the ladies into the dining room and guided them to a pair of seats before they'd had a moment to protest.

"Cec, mate, why do you have to go vampirising the fun out of any great get-together?" Andrea scoffed.

"It's just his way, Andrea. We can't expect him to be any less high-strung anymore than we can expect James to be an upstanding and respectable member of society." Essie shrugged, bringing the ladies some cool water to their place settings.

"She does have a point, there." Susan chuckled.

Some knocking came at the front door, drawing the group's attention. Cecil turned his attention to Andrea with a derisive grin on his face.

"Knocking. At the door. *Fancy that!*" He chided as he left the dining room. Andrea stuck out her tongue at the back of his head with a laugh as she lounged back into her seat. In no time, Spencer and Amelia Cole entered with Cecil close behind. The butler was deliberately guiding the youngish professor, as his nose was buried in a journal.

"*Bonjour à tous!*" Mrs Cole chimed as she placed her worn-out fedora hat on Cecil's head, to his annoyance. "Oh, Cecil, take my jacket too. *Terriblement chaud*, dreadful warm."

"Which is saying something, for England." Cecil sighed as he removed Amelia's maroon blazer. "And keep the cigars stored, please."

"*Oui, oui*, Cecil." Mrs Cole nodded with a wave of her hand. She had come in a maroon suit paired with a blue vest and a striped brocade tie. Her shining black hair was perfectly styled, as always, and her large brown eyes slid over to her barely observant husband. "*Cher.*" She placed her hand on Spencer's journal and lowered it a bit, finally drawing his attention.

"Oh, sorry darling. I just have a few more-" Spencer jolted a bit, removing his pince-nez glasses upon observing his surroundings. "When did we arrive at Everjust?" The entire room filled with laughter as the couple took their seats. The Professor had only a simple Herringbone suit on with a bowtie and tattersall shirt. As simple and well put together as his clothing was, his sandy hair remained a finger-combed mess which framed his soft facial features.

"I take it you're hard at work on some research, Spencer?" Andrea chuckled.

"Indeed, I'm looking into a theory on Woolley's recent discoveries at Ur. According to the findings, apparently, the daily life of the common folk may not have been far and away different from our own! In fact, they found the remains of what looked like an ordinary neighbourhood of homes and shops and-" Spencer began rambling, to which Amelia would normally admire him, but she could see Andrea's eyes begin to glaze over. The art museum owner pulled her husband into a deep passionate kiss which made him fall limp in his seat with an expression like a stunned animal.

"*Désolé mon amour*, but this is not the university." She smiled.

"Q-quite right... yes." Spencer shook off his adulation-induced stupor, nearly losing his glasses in the process. He removed them and dropped them into the breast pocket of his jacket. "Anywho, what's new with the two of you, Susan?"

"Oh, not much really. I've simply been enjoying some new books, however, Andrea has discovered a new radio program she enjoys quite a bit." Susan explained, keeping the environment alive.

"Oh?" Amelia's expression lit up. She adored the radio. "*Dis-le*, Andrea, do tell!"

"It's right up our alley, a murder mystery program!" This gripped the table's attention. "It's called *Death Before Dawn*, and it's like listening to an entire mystery novella in three-part serials!"

"Time! What's the time?" Amelia urged, tapping her wristwatch.

"It's a late-night program that broadcasts, oh, 'round ten." Susan added, having caught a bit from time to time.

"Oh, lovely." Cecil rolled his eyes. "Something else to distract Miss Cyrus. She'll never get *any* sleep now." The butler checked his watch again. "Lunch is already late. If Roland doesn't get here with James in the next five minutes-"

"Unwind your springs a bit, Cecil, we're right here!" Came the cheerful bellow of Mr Wood from the back of the kitchen.

"And about time!" Cecil yelled back with a small stamp of his heel. Essie pushed open the kitchen door to see the two men, one gentleman and one being smacked with a wooden spoon by Cook.

"Stay out of that, you!" Cook scolded James as he attempted to take a bit of dough from some cookie batter.

"Ow!" The American philanderer, James Mondey, jumped to the side in a vain attempt to avoid the spoon.

"Out, out, out, the both of ya!" Cook shooed both men into the dining room. "Essie, luv, come grab the lunch."

Essie trotted over to the kitchen to aid Cook while James and Mr Wood stood aside to stay out of her way once she came in with the food.

"Well! Hello, everyone!" Mr Wood bellowed into the room with a clap of his hands while Cecil pulled a chair out for him at the head of the table with his foot. "It does my heart good to see you all together again!"

"Going out truly hasn't been the same without you, Jimmy!" Andrea chimed in. James playfully rolled his eyes as he hated being referred to as '*Jimmy*'.

To everyone's befuddlement, Mr Wood guided James into the head seat. Normally, *nobody* sat there except for the master of the house. Whatever James had to say must be truly important if it warranted having the central seat!

"I can't express the happiness I feel being back here, Andy," James replied to the sultry flapper. "Visiting home is always such a drudgery and if there's anything I like more than globetrotting to exotic places, it's bringing a sense of intrigue to this academic burg!"

"And what is it you've brought to our '*academic burg*', James?" Professor Cole chimed in.

"Well, to explain that, I have to journey back to what my wretched family had to tell me during my stay." James paused momentarily as the food was being served. Upon the plates of Hamburg steak with assorted steamed vegetables being dispersed, the staff took their own seats and awaited James's story. "To put it simply, my family is sick of me embarrassing them for my own benefit. So they're cutting me off." He shrugged indifferently while the rest of the Criminology Society stopped dead in the middle of their meals!

"That's terrible, *mon ami*!" Amelia threw her hands up. "While you may be promiscuous, it is *them* that should be ashamed of themselves!"

"She's right, I've met your family," Susan interjected clutching her metaphorical pearls. "They really are the most ghastly people!"

"Eh, true, but they're also fools that believe their word is an infallible bond." James gave a sly chuckle as though he was up to some mischief.

"He's been impish like this the entire time since I've picked him up." Mr Wood gave his beard a scratch. Everyone waited in rapt attention for what else James had to say, as this was iffy news and his letter made it sound so urgent! What could possibly have happened to change his demeanour?

"They've foolishly given me a chance to do right and give them a headline that doesn't bring a pall on their egos." James chuckled. "I have to host some sort of *proper* event."

"Then you are definitely doomed." Andrea sighed. "The only event you've ever hosted was an orgy."

"Ah, but I think I've got the perfect idea and it will, in theory, be beneficial to several of us!" James seemed confident. Everyone awaited the suggestion. "A smithing competition!" And with that, the room fell silent. Looks of confusion drew across everyone's faces. The silence in the room was deafening.

"Um, James?" Professor Cole broke the deadly quiet. "How is a smithing competition to save your liberal income?"

"*C'est l'idée la plus absurde dont j'ai jamais entendu parler.*" Amelia rubbed her temple as she mumbled about the absurdity of his scheme.

"I'm aware that the suggestion seems unconventional, but I have several points to make on the subject." James tried to quell the confusion. "Firstly, it will be a grand and unusual spectacle to bring the greater community together." He entwined his fingers to illustrate his point. "A novelty for people to enjoy the unseen work of meticulous labour; Second, in addition to seeing the work of said blacksmiths, we'll present them with challenges to recreate some authentic historical pieces, such as swords of various designs!" This part of James's suggestion aroused Professor Cole's intrigue, prompting the androgynous academic to stroke his bowtie in thought. "Third, I think it could create a better awareness for an otherwise forgotten art that industrialisation has overshadowed but *not* replaced." James turned to Mr Wood, who was sitting stoic but had a clear twinkle in his eye as he loved to consider the roots of all business. "And finally, Mr Wood, I hope I can count on you for this one."

"Oh?" Mr Wood's grin began to show.

"The grand winner of this spectacle could perhaps earn a place working for the esteemed Mr Roland Wood?" James shrugged, a coy expression plastered over his face.

"Aha! *That's* why you were so enigmatic in the car!" Mr Wood laughed, his deep voice almost rattling the table. "I say, this idea is just mad enough to work!"

"Well, it's mad alright," Andrea added. "But, what the hell, I'll support it." She waved her hand.

"As will I." Susan clapped her hands, her excitement renewed.

"I know you have won my husband over on the idea." Amelia inched her seat over and leaned on Spencer's shoulder who nodded vigorously.

"Then it's settled! I knew I could count on my closest friends to help me coordinate this!" James continued his meal, as did the rest of the Society.

Mr Wood always enjoyed finding a way that he could give to people gainfully. James's idea was odd, true, but inspired. He laughed in his mind at the thought of how much rum James likely ingested to come up with it. It was wonderful to have him back locally, since things seemed slightly dry, even when the rest of the Criminology Society came together. James always had something to inject the right amount of chaos to liven things up.

Everything else aside, this was going to be an interesting undertaking. Starting tomorrow, the Criminology Society begin sponsoring the Mondey Smith's Exhibition!

...title pending.

Chapter Two

Two months of expedited work and preparations later and in under a week, the day would soon be here! To everyone's surprise, James took on a great deal of the work himself. Coordinating the competition had been his only objective for the entire duration, working closely with the rest of the Society and their contacts. That said, James still left plenty of time to keep his wits sharp with an excess of alcohol—the only person in history to think better while inebriated.

James was currently at the University Park enjoying a celebratory tipple as Mr Wood came over to sit beside him on a park bench that had a perfect view of the surrounding area. Booths had been erected by many local businesses, both confectionary and creative alike! James's assumption that this event of his would be good for the locals was spot on, as there was a mix of favourite locations being represented here as well as some far less known people attempting to widen their scope.

"You should be proud of yourself, James." Mr Wood twiddled his moustache.

"I usually am." James replied with an amused smirk.

Both men peered across the site set up in the University Parks. As mentioned before, booths, demonstrations, and concessions from green to green! The hard work had paid off in droves as people across Oxford were only talking about the spectacle as of late. As the old adage goes, build it and they will come. James was correct that people would want to see the old art of smithing in action. Professor Cole often said that humans are naturally curious creatures. The entire event managed to fill itself with other artistic feats such as glass blowing and more!

"Come, James. Let's check the competition area before the main event comes around, eh?" Mr Wood bid James to follow.

"Right, you are, old man." The younger gent downed the rest of his drink and followed.

They both crossed the grassy park and through the crowds of people as they made their way to the cordoned-off section that they'd designated for the competition ground.

"So about your friends at Sanderson's-" James began.

"Sander and *Son's*," Mr Wood corrected his young friend. "It's just Sander here today. And yes, I ensured they supplied us with the necessary equipment."

"Good. I'll take your word for it if everything looks right." James gave the bridge of his nose a scratch. "You'd know better than me."

Upon reaching the area, the two men saw a familiar face they didn't expect. Spencer Cole was awaiting them along with the elder Mr Sander. James tilted his head, surprised to see the professor.

"Professor!" Mr Wood clapped, happy but just as confused to see him. "What brings you here today?"

"Well, as I was asked to be one of the judges for this event, I was eager to get a closer look at the types of forges we would be seeing in use up close." Spencer twiddled his fingers.

"The lad needs a lid." Mr Sander grumbled, referencing Professor Cole's tendency to ramble on.

"Trust me, we know." James laughed at Spencer's puzzled expression.

"Well, come along with us." Mr Wood rattled Spencer's shoulder. "We want a look at the equipment ourselves. Mr Sander?" The older working man was obliged to follow. "By the by, how is your son?"

"His recovery has progressed considerably, thank you for asking. He'll be back to work in a few weeks 'cording to the doc." Mr Sander took the three into the area where several large stations were placed in sequential equidistance. "We had to call in a few favours to procure the actual forges, but most of the rest of the equipment we supplied ourselves." He began to explain as they approached the first workstation.

"Even the anvils?" Spencer inquired.

"You'd be surprised how much our ordinary building work requires them, schoolboy." Mr Sander nodded. "We got something mighty fine to keep the heat up on these things as well. Better than fighting a billow." The old man began cranking a handle on the side of the massive oven that let out the sound of a fan beneath where the fire of the forge would be!

"Clever!" James exclaimed. "Part of me wants to light this thing up to see it in action!" Spencer nodded in agreement.

"*No*, sirs." Mr Wood held back both overeager men.

"Wood's right, we already tested this stuff and I don't trust a couple of wild-eyed lads like you around it." Sander swatted James's hand away.

"What about the tools?" Spencer inquired, taking note of the empty tool rack.

"Oh, we only wanted people who knew what they were doing. Professionals, you understand." James explained. "The contestants will be providing their own tools."

"I can understand that. When I'm on a dig site, I require the use of my familiar pieces." Spencer nodded, fiddling with his tie again.

"It's ingenious." Mr Wood patted the machinery. "I'm eager to see this spectacle." He then looked off to the side to see a modestly dressed woman approaching. "Speaking of, another of our judges is approaching!"

The three men left Sander to continue his work as they met up with the woman at the edge of the competition area. She was older with her hair neatly done and showing portions of grey. A modest yet well-kept day dress was how she clothed herself and it showed her stocky arms. Whoever this woman was, she was clearly a hard worker!

"Miss Clubb!" Mr Wood shouted out. "A pleasure to meet you face to face at last!"

"And I take it you must be Mr Wood?" The woman held out her hand and gripped Mr Wood's firmly.

"I am indeed. Boys, this is Annie Clubb." He introduced the woman to James and Spencer. "This woman is the *only* famous female blacksmith in all of England!"

"A lady blacksmith?" James queried.

"Problem, sir?" Asked Annie.

"Hardly! I'm astonished in the best possible way!" The sly young man gleefully stated. "I couldn't have asked for a more unique judge for this event! No offence, Professor."

"None taken, James. I, myself, am fascinated by the diverse range in this field of work." Spencer was fascinated by the prospect of having someone who wasn't likely to belittle him for not being what one might call a '*man's man*'.

"Aye, my work is predominantly in iron decor, suchlike balcony framing and other decorative works, but I like to think I've got a pretty discerning eye for detail." Annie explained. "Also, I'm far from the *only* lady smith in England. There have been several entries from lady metalworkers."

"Quite true! And I look forward to conferring with you, Miss Clubb. Spencer Cole, Professor of Archaeological History at the university." Spencer winced upon shaking hands with the strongarmed woman. Annie laughed and turned to James.

"And are you the event's host?" James nodded in reply to the woman. "I hope this won't insult you but you don't look as though you've ever worked hard in your life."

"So why am I holding this sort of event?" James chuckled, predicting her train of thought. "Well, full transparency, it's not only about the underappreciated art but also about saving my lucrative allowance from my stuck-up family." Spencer and Mr Wood peered between the two in hopes this would not turn Annie Clubb away. To their relief, she smiled.

"I can appreciate the honesty, young man. And I can also appreciate calling smithing an underappreciated art." She seemed pleased with what she'd heard. "Now, if you'll excuse me, I'd like to take in more of the surroundings."

"I shall join you, if I may. I can take you to your lodgings after, first class all the way!" Mr Wood followed along. James teasingly let out a suggestive whistle, prompting a roll of the eyes from Mr Wood.

"So, Spencer, where's Amelia?"

"Back at the museum. I came here for a bit of an impromptu visit." The Professor explained.

"*And* you wanted to satiate your curiosity for the builds, huh?" James patted his friend's shoulder.

"Indeed. How many contestants do we need to choose? I've quite forgotten." Spencer jumped directly to his next curiosity.

"Six! Six lucky individuals who just might be winning a position in Mr Wood's employ." James clapped his hands together...

A man in a fine pinstripe suit took notice of the conversation between the two men and stroked the whiskers on his chin. The figure then blended into the crowd of curious onlookers, seeming to enjoy the surrounding events himself. Spencer looked over his shoulder.

"Okay there?" James asked.

"Yes, just thought something was a bit off for a moment. Never mind it." Spencer shrugged.

James and Spencer threaded themselves through the crowd at the park entrance. Spencer wasn't one for being surrounded by large crowds of people, but having James close by was something of a relief. The two discussed more details of the event over some cheaply made fried confections that one of the booths was testing out until Spencer began reeling into one of his history-based tangents which James *pretended* to understand. The Professor could see the glazed look in James's eye, similar to Andrea's.

"You see, James?" Spencer sighed. He nodded in faux understanding. Spencer could tell that James was passively listening to him, and so, decided he would have a bit of *fun* with him. "In addition, I believe I've discovered a long-lost civilization of mole men under the country-side who can help us build a spaceship to the moon."

"Now that *would* be-wait, *what!?*" James shook off his dazed presence of mind, having only caught the 'mole men' portion of the outlandish statement.

"Haha!" Professor Cole couldn't contain his amusement. "I think you'd best head back to Everjust. We all have an early day tomorrow."

"True enough, friend. I'll confer with you then." James patted Professor Cole on the shoulder and left the event.

James began flagging down a taxicab to take him back. He assumed Mr Wood would already have gone home, but if not, he did not want to shorten his fun. As the cab came to a halt in front of him, James opened the back door but froze when caught sight of someone in the corner of his eye, near the entrance. He thought he saw a familiar woman in the distance but she'd disappeared into the crowd, if she was even there in the first place.

"Mate? Where to, I said?" The cabbie asked with his teeth clenched on a cigarette.

"Oh! Uh, Holywell Street, my good man." James continued into the car and rode in uncharacteristic silence. He hoped he was extremely wrong about who he thought he saw at that park. His thoughts were so deep that he didn't even realize when the cab turned onto the requested street and came to a stop only a few doors down from Everjust.

"Oi! Mate! Holywell Street, alright?" The cabbie snapped his fingers.

"Ah, right! Here you are." James paid the driver and exited the cab.

"Yanks." The cabbie huffed and drove off, leaving James to finish walking to the Society's home.

James found himself focusing less on the potential sighting and walked his way to the front door of Everjust. He opened the door to find Essie waiting for him with a glass of scotch.

"Efficient as ever, Essie!" James laughed.

"I aim to please!" She beamed at James.

"Careful, or I may take you up *further* on that statement." James winked as he took the glass. He was then struck on the head with a newspaper as he approached the entrance to the sitting room.

"Have some respect for the lady, Mondey." Cecil snapped.

"Lighten up, you automaton, it was a joke." James smoothed his hair. He sat down in one of the chairs, arching his legs over the arm. Cecil's face went red. "So did either of you make it out to see the fairground?"

"I did. Cecil was uninterested at the time," Essie explained. "But I've talked him into joining me for the competition."

"Is that so?" James peered at Cecil as he finished his drink. The butler's face had been relieved of its rouge everywhere but his cheeks. Suddenly the strike on his head wasn't so unwarranted.

"Have you already met the contestants?" Essie asked.

"Personally? No, we just had people send in an entry piece and I had Spencer and Mr Wood do the examining." James scratched at his ear. "I'm not one for detailed art unless it's a nice car, a fine woman, or a decorative decanter if you catch my drift."

"I suppose you enjoyed the glass blower booth at the event, then?" Essie giggled.

"Naturally!" James finished his drink and placed the glass on the side table.

"Finished?" Cecil asked with a bend in his waist.

"Yes, I think one will suffice until after dinner." James agreed.

"Good." Cecil then unceremoniously slapped James's legs off of the arm of the chair. "Didn't want any spillage on the upholstery."

"Point made, damn." James laughed, knowing he was poking the bear.

The sound of the door opening and closing rather roughly roused everyone's attention. Heavy footsteps in fine shoe leather made it clear that it was Mr Wood arriving home as well... and he was upset about something.

"Mr Wood?" Essie asked as he went by the opening to the sitting room. He was grumbling to himself about something or other.

"Roland?" Cecil raised his brow and followed him into the hall. He snapped his fingers which drew the massive man's attention.

"Oh, Cecil. Good." Mr Wood handed his butler the hat that was on his head and stroked his beard. "James here?"

"In here, old boy!" James called, still seated in the armchair.

Mr Wood entered the sitting room and sat rather heavily on the couch adjacent to James's seat. He sighed angrily and leaned back, pulling down at his vest to adjust it for seating.

"My friend, if we decide to hold another event of this sort, we *must* be more selective of those allowed to attend." Everyone was perplexed, as it wasn't like Mr Wood to have an exclusive mentality.

"What do you mean, pal?" James pulled a bit on the thread of information.

"I mean, *I'm* not the only headhunter that's attending." Mr Wood growled. "Some fellow from a company called Majority Armes is passing cards about to metal workers."

"Majority Armes? I'm unfamiliar." James thought. Mr Wood handed a business card over to James and the young man's face reflected the realization of why Mr Wood was so bothered.

"What is it, James?" Essie tried to take a look herself. James simply showed her.

Majority Armes
Weapons Manufacturer and
Defensive Solutions

Essie cocked her head, unsure of what to make of this. Seeing James's realization and the look of aggravation on Mr Wood's face, it began to make sense. In hindsight, it should have been quite obvious from the moment she looked at the card.

"I see." She replied.

"I *despise* weapons developers." Mr Wood growled. "All they do is profit off the suffering of others. While I don't deny that arms can be a necessity, defence and protection are the *last* things on *those* sorts of minds. Merely the profit that can be made by *causing* the most suffering."

"Steady on, Roland, else you'll plague yourself with the war again." Cecil sighed, his shoulders uncharacteristically relaxed.

"The Great War always plagues me, Cecil, just drop it." Mr Wood replied rather curtly.

The room dropped into an awkward silence. James knew Mr Wood was right and was kicking himself for not considering that undesirable developers might attempt to arrive. However, it was also foolish to think they could regulate the backgrounds of people arriving at a free festive event.

"I'm going to check on Cook." Essie broke the silence. "She should be starting dinner soon."

"Good thinking, Essie." Mr Wood's mood changed instantly to his normal cheer. It was clearly forced, but it snapped him out of thinking about sad or bad things.

James wanted to ask Mr Wood some further questions about this representative and the possibility of kicking him out of the event if he's spotted. He didn't think it prudent to bring anything else up that might upset his friend further. Besides which, how could they ask him to leave if he hadn't *actually* done anything wrong? Throwing out an undesirable for arbitrary reasons is something James's family would do, which made his stomach turn. His drifting mind was anchored back to the waking world by another drink being held in front of his face.

"Ah, thanks." James graciously took it from the stoic butler.

"I think I'll take one of those, myself, Cecil." Mr Wood stood up and walked over to the decanter. "I'm not going to let this upstart pistol-pusher ruin my day *or* this event!"

"Quite right, Roland." Mr Blackbird nodded. "Given the choice between you and some dime-a-dozen weapon maker, anyone with a minimum effort mind would find that choice easy."

"Here here!" Mr Wood raised his glass before having a swig. He looked at James, who still seemed lost in his own mind. "James." He snapped his fingers. A lot of that going around today.

"Eh?" James rubbed his eyes. "It's nothing. I just need to rest up for the event tomorrow. After dinner, I think I'll turn in."

"Hm. Something's definitely wrong with you." Mr Wood stated. James tried to feign innocence with a shrug.

"He's right." Essie reentered the room. "Turning in early, no nightly escapades with groups of attractive people, it's not like you at all!"

"Okay!" James threw up his hands and laughed uncomfortably. "You know I love you all... except you, you're a bit prickly," He pointed at Cecil who narrowed his eyes at him. "But I am *not* going to be interrogated on one little deviation from my erratic routine!"

Everyone just stood there in an awkward silence. Essie and Cecil had never seen James flare his temper before. Mr Wood, however, had. He knew exactly what triggers these kinds of tempers.

"Very well, James." Mr Wood nodded as he subtly glanced at Essie and Cecil and waved his hands to have them back off of James. "We'll push you no further. Just know that we're all here to help whenever you need."

"Yes, sorry." James felt immediate regret for snapping at them. "I just hope that we'll be able to have a great time this very week. *Nothing* is going to spoil it for us if I have anything to say about it."

James's explanation satisfied Mr Wood, since he understood why. It satisfied Cecil because he wasn't that invested in James's internal struggles. Essie, however, was dangerously curious as to what could possibly make this eccentric playboy act like a brooding normal man. It was unsettling, and it was also a mystery. And mysteries are what the Criminology Society are all about.

Chapter Three

The day finally came and James seemed to be in better spirits! The whole Society had arrived at the event's opening and spent the entire time being merry as the various artisans peddled their craft! The sense of community was beautiful to see, and Mr Wood loved to see people *create* what they love. James was right. Whoever would win this contest would be someone he would find to be a *pleasure* to work with. Cecil and Essie were on either side of the large man. Essie was enjoying the sights, but Cecil was scanning the crowd for anyone who looked like a headhunter for a weapons dealer. If he could catch the man and eject him from the event on James's behalf, it may save Mr Wood a great deal of unrest.

"Mr Wood!" Susan called out. She and Andrea approached the trio. The ladies were dressed well with candyfloss in their hands. Susan gave Essie a short hug, careful not to get her sweet into the maid's hair. "This place is amazing!"

"Isn't it!?" Essie agreed fervently.

"A worker's wonderland, wouldn't you say?" Mr Wood chuckled jovially.

"Have you seen Jimmy?" Andrea chimed in. "We've looked all over."

"Ah, I believe he's having a little confab with the chosen contestants. I couldn't very well be there for it myself, or the secret grand prize might be given away!" Mr Wood patted his chest proudly.

"Funny." Andrea mused with a mouth full of cotton candy.

"Attention, attention everyone!" James's voice sang above the crowd from a microphone. "All those who wish to see a phenomenal spectacle of human creativity and ingenuity, please approach the stage for a special announcement!"

The Society members followed the crowd of people to the rigged-up stage set in front of the cordoned area that SanderSon's had built. Behind the oversized podium were six individuals stationed at each of the forges.

One was a burly man who was clearly experienced in this type of work from the state of his hands and shirt. The next person was very clean-cut and confident, wearing a nice shirt and vest while flashing around his pristine and well-maintained tools as he basked in the crowd's attention. Another was a very gorgeous woman in slightly bedraggled clothes, the type *meant* for working. The person at the forge furthest back was a smaller man who was preoccupied with taking inventory of his equipment like a true professional. The penultimate was a red-haired fellow of average build and burns that trailed up his left arm, and similar yet smaller scars on his right as he rolled his sleeves up. The final contestant was another woman, very tall with her hair tied tight and her shoulders broad, looking like a younger Miss Clubb.

"An impressive collection of craftspersons." Mr Wood stroked his beard as he took in the view.

Everyone's attention was drawn back to James's podium after he inadvertently caused a bit of feedback. The crowd, and he, winced.

"Sorry folks." A laugh rolled across the crowd. "Now, as I was saying, we are very pleased to bring you a one-of-a-kind experience to see behind the veil of dangerous and artisanal metalwork! Watch as these six professionals build the historic items requested of them before your very eyes. The greatest of whom, will also be winning a supremely grand prize! Before we begin, I would like to introduce these amazing artists!" James turned on his heel to point them each out. For ease of understanding, the following shall be listed in order of their description above. "May I present, Emanuel Hammond, a farrier by trade, keeping your horses on their toes!" His boisterous laugh was joined by the crowd. "Michael Tilmann, a gear maker who designs the fineries to keep you running on time! I'm looking at you there, Cecil Blackbird!" He pointed at the stiff butler who wrenched his hands behind his back as the Society members laughed at his expense.

"Come now, Cecil, that was funny!" Essie chuckled as she took his arm.

"Next we have the lovely Miss Sara Ware, peddling her namesake as a smith of intricate and *decorative* metalwork, not unlike one of our judges!" James bowed, gesturing over to Miss Clubb at the edge of the crowd. "And next, Jefferey Lane, who seems to be a little distracted today." Mr Lane was still taking inventory of his setup but waved absentmindedly to the crowd, signifying that he heard his name. "The young man is a knifemaker who creates phenomenal skinning knives for the hunt!" James looked at the man with the burns. "Kent McClain, a smith of *many* things, so I'm told! You ask it, he'll make it. Ask and he can't make it, you didn't need it anyhow!" James rubbed his hands together. "And finally, without further ado, our final contestant. The lady, Jaquelin Brush! Another farrier, but can also straighten out the body of your motorcar," He looked at the built woman and bit his lip a moment in a specific *interest.* "likely with her bare hands!"

"Oh, James." Susan sighed with a palm to her face.

"So without further ado! One of our judges, the esteemed Professor Cole, will pose the first challenge to our aforementioned contestants! Enjoy!" James removed himself from the podium and shook Spencer's hand as he approached with a sword in hand.

"Hello all," Spencer spoke meekly into the microphone. "I have in my hand, an authentic Celtic chieftain sword. Known as a symbol of authority, notice the hilt made in the shape of a human effigy. Now, the first challenge is to create a blade of your choice, it can be *any* type, but in order to see your creative arts we want you to craft a similar hilt in this fashion." Spencer held the sword up carefully for all to see. "We judges will be wandering between the workstations to review your methods but feel free to approach this sword as necessary as it will be on display between the forges." Spencer removed himself and approached a table with a display rack situated exactly where he'd said.

James joined with Mr Wood and the others with a cheery smile on his face. He rubbed his hands together as he watched the smiths approach the sword to examine their objective.

"You have brought together an impressive group of people, James." Mr Wood nodded.

"Can't stand that Tilmann fellow." James's smile turned to an incredulous smirk. Everyone glanced at him.

"Well, *that's* a bit out of the blue." Andrea commented on his churlish attitude.

"Eh, there's just something about that man that rubs me the wrong way. He's very showy and cavalier." James explained. Everyone held back some laughter.

"So he is like you, then?" Cecil raised an amused smirk due to vocalising everyone's thoughts at the moment. James winked an eye at him, frustrated.

"*No.*" James placed his hands in his pockets. "I mean he's arrogant. The guy was boasting so much about his work that he was telling the others to just give up and declare him the winner of the special prize." Mr Wood's face sank as well after hearing James's explanation.

"Hm." That was all Mr Wood had said on the matter as he watched all of the smiths approach their work-stations.

"Hope the bloke dirties up that poncy vest of his." Andrea huffed.

"Indeed. His arrogance shows in the way he presents himself here." Cecil added. "He may be dressed smart, but he looks the least professional of the bunch. Person-ally, I like that Jefferey chap."

"Because *he's* like *you?*" James chided, nudging the uptight butler.

"I hardly think *you're* one to disparage someone else's character James." Another American voice, that of a woman, came from behind.

James's expression changed to one of dismal disdain as they all turned to face the woman. She was in a glam-orous silk dress with a string of fine pearls and a wide asymmetrical hat. She looked like some villainess from a suspense serial.

"I knew I'd seen you here." James sneered. "I felt the icy chill of your presence when I was on my way back to Everjust the other day. Surprising I didn't feel it the moment you arrived in England."

"How could anyone feel anything *but* a chill in this stale old tomb of a town?" The woman gave a haughty laugh as though she'd made a clever quip. No one else was laughing.

"James?" Essie inquired. "Who is this?"

"My meretricious sister." James rolled his eyes. "What are you doing here in Oxford, Elsbeth?"

"Father wanted me to attend the event that you decided to hold." Elsbeth Mondey grinned with a sickeningly snide manner about her. "Just to ensure that you truly aren't bringing more shame on the Mondey name." She looked around. "I can't say that *I'm* impressed, brother dear. A *smithing* competition? *Ha!*"

"Nobody asked your opinion, Elsbeth." James brushed his nose. "And do you ever bathe in anything besides an overabundance of cheap perfume?" Elsbeth's expression sank but her disparaging smile remained.

"I *have* to give a few extra spritzes for a backwater like *this*. And it's thirteen dollars per ounce, so *hardly* cheap." She flourished her hand as she glanced at the ladies in the group, apparently trying to admonish them in her own favour.

"The people seem to enjoy the exposition, Miss. Isn't that what matters?" Essie chimed in. Elsbeth glanced at Essie's less expensive clothing.

"James, who is this and is she important?" She refused to acknowledge Essie until she knew if she was anywhere near her class to even talk to. It made Essie shuffle back, self-conscious.

"She's important to *me*." James crossed his arms.

"Oh, so '*no*', then." Elsbeth smirked as she shooed Essie away without another word. "I sent father some correspondence and he hardly even believed what I'd told him because he didn't trust that you even knew *hard work* like smithing even existed."

"As though *you* do?" James rolled his eyes and laughed at the absurdity. "So the only reason you're here is to be a foil for me and taunt the loss of my familial income?"

"I have to entertain myself, don't I?" Elsbeth smiled.

"Well, *ahem*," Mr Wood finally added in. "I believe that you shall be sorely disappointed since this event has garnered the attention of all of Oxford. To say nothing of the spotlight this is shining on an otherwise under-appreciated profession."

"Oh, sir," Elsbeth shook her head condescendingly. "You know you are respected in our family, but Roland-"

"*Mr Wood to you!*" The entire group asserted simultaneously. Elsbeth was taken aback.

Mr Wood is not one to force respect by calling him '*Mister*', but respect is something that is earned on a two-way street. He knew the members of the Mondey family and while he does have land dealings with them in the States, the only member of the family to have his respect is James. This spoiled little upstart was *not* going to call him a familiar name as though they were old friends. Only one person on this earth calls Mr Wood, Roland, and it most certainly was not going to be *her*.

Elsbeth was stunned that anyone, especially the two *help*, would speak to her like that. She'd have come back at them, except their ruckus had just been drowned out by a very thunderous sound, followed by the crowd's combined gasps and screams! They all turned to see what had prompted such a stir and they were stunned to see that Jefferey Lane's forge had exploded! Moreover, not only was his body lying limp and charred across the anvil of his station, but Spencer was sprawled out, frighteningly near to the exploded forge!

"Spencer!" Susan screamed, dropping her sweet treat as the group all ran into the divided area.

Miss Clubb managed to drag the professor away from the ruined equipment as everyone approached. James came sliding next to Spencer, without a care for the state of his suit, and began checking his chest. The professor's lapels and vest were singed, meaning he was standing fairly close when the explosion happened.

"Is he alright!?" Essie knelt down beside James, panicked but attempting to keep her head. Something Susan was having trouble doing as Andrea held onto her.

"He's fine. Just knocked out." James turned his attention to Mr Lane's charred body where Mr Wood and Emanuel were using their jacket and apron, respectively, to swat out the excess flames around the forge. "The same cannot be said for Jefferey!"

"I should say not." Mr Wood panted as he backed away.

"We should ph-phone the f-f-ire brig-gade." Susan sputtered, trying to regain control of her torrential emotions.

"Pretty sure they heard the explosion for themselves, Miss." Andrea shrugged while rubbing Susan's shoulder. "Likely the police as well."

"Wow. Seems we just can't have nice things anymore." James sighed. "I'm not waiting for the ambulance, I'm getting Spence to the hospital this minute." Mr Wood grabbed James's shoulder.

"I'll take care of him. *You'll* need to give the statements." He stated. "You're the host here, after all." Mr Wood scooped up the professor and made his way toward the crowd. He momentarily scanned the wide range of people and staggered a moment when he noticed something odd. A man in a dark suit, bearded, who seemed much less concerned with what had just transpired than everyone else in the park. The man seemed to take notice that he was being watched and slunk back into the crowd. Mr Wood was too busy taking care of his friend to worry about catching the representative from Majority Armes.

In the meantime, James was pacing in front of the stage awaiting the authorities, who were near at hand by the sound of the approaching sirens. James crossed his fingers that the arriving officer would be who he thought. Thankfully, he was most correct as he saw Inspector Gabriel Daniels making his way into the park with a handful of officers at his side. He began directing them until he came to a stunned stop.

"Ah... The Criminology Society." Inspector Daniels sighed, greeting the collective group. "Why, pray tell, am I not surprised?"

"Nice to see you again, too, Gabe." James flourished his hand.

"I was told there was an explosion, not that I needed to be. The panic that it caused could be heard from my desk." Daniels walked past James and looked over at the ruined forge. "Jiminy, that's a rough way to go."

"Pretty sure it didn't hurt long." Andrea pointed out.

"Quite right." Daniels approached and began examining the body. "Victim's name?"

"Jefferey Lane, knife maker. He was in the process of building an effigy sword for our competition." James explained.

"Not an amateur then. That's certainly someone who would know how to make a blade without a dangerous mistake." Daniels glanced inside the misshapen stove and noticed something interesting. He removed his coat and covered his hands to reach in.

"My, that poor coat." James mused.

"Coats are cheap, lives are not." Daniels yanked out a horrible-looking chunk of metal. "This doesn't look much like a sword."

"It's a crucible." Cecil stepped up and leaned close to the metal. "Notice the separations from the outside and inside layers of metal. He was using the crucible method to create a strong blade, possibly with a pattern that would stand out."

"It stood out alright." Daniels nodded. "Seems that something inside of the crucible itself caused the explosion."

"But all he put in was the raw metal. I saw it myself." Essie added. Daniels acknowledged her but was deep in thought.

"Not exclusively, it seems." Daniels took notice of an unmarked box of white powder in the tool rack. "Constable!" He called out. An officer came as ordered. "Take this and have the metal tested for any sort of explosive materials."

"Aye, sir." The constable carried away the damaged pseudo-weapon in question.

"Mr Mondey?" Daniels turned back to James and the group. "Was there anything you'd seen? Anything suspicious?"

"Afraid not, old boy. I was preoccupied with preparing my introduction to the competition. Each of the contestants was in charge of checking their own forges before the event was to begin." The amiable American explained. "The judges were close at hand during the building portion."

"And where were you at the time?" Daniels asked, genuinely curious. "Weren't you watching as well?"

"I confess I was a little distracted by the sudden appearance of my *sister*." Daniels took notice of the slight sneer in James's voice.

"Not a functional family dynamic, I take it?" He asked.

"Unimportant." James waved his hand as though he was trying to waft away the terrible stench of this subject. "Ultimately, you would need to ask the judges. One of whom has been taken to hospital."

"Which one?" Daniels stroked his smooth chin.

"Professor Cole, I'm afraid." The Inspector was taken aback when James mentioned this. "I think he is fine, but he took quite a shock. He was only a couple of feet away when the forge exploded, if that."

"Perfect. Now I'll have Mrs Cole breathing down my neck to find who did this." Daniels sighed. He turned to the other members of the Society. "Any of you see any thing of consequence?"

"Afraid not, Inspector." Susan shook her head.

"Very well. I'll need you to help anyway, Mr Mondey." Daniels gestured him to follow. "I want to speak to the contestants *and* your judges."

"Righto." James agreed and the two were off."

The group shuffled uncomfortably as they watched the two men saunter off to speak with the other smiths. Andrea rubbed her hands together with an anxiety that she didn't usually have. Not the same as her mistress's but a restless one. A need for action. Essie picked up on it and felt the same. As always in these situations, Essie's need for closure was vast and someone she cared about was harmed, intensifying her drive.

"Should we follow?" The petite maid asked. Her over-wrought superior tried to maintain a stoic demeanour, but the nervous fondling of his timepiece betrayed his emotions.

"Not likely. Inspector Daniels would likely get hacked off at the intrusion." Cecil pointed out with a flick of his watch.

"I... I would l-like to go to the hosp-pital and see if Spencer is alright." Susan wrung her handkerchief that she kept in the collar of her blouse. Andrea agreed but Essie was still eager to find a way to be of use.

"You go ahead, *I* still want to find some answers," Essie spoke low. "I want to try and find that executive from the weapons manufacturer." She was filled with a determination that made Cecil nervous.

"We should either head back to Everjust or visit the Professor in the hospital." He stated. "Your choice."

"If you really want to keep an eye on me, then join me. But I *will* stay and find out if Majority Armes has anything to do with this." Essie had her arms crossed which, amusingly, made her look like a pouting child, but the intensity of her stare was enough to make Cecil realize that if he wanted to keep her safe, there was only one option.

"Ugh... If one can't beat them, join them, eh?" He sighed heavily.

"If you like." Essie winked at him cheekily which infuriated Cecil on the inside but entertained the others.

With that, the party split into three groups to get to the bottom of the latest situation. Once again, death has been brought to the proverbial doorstep of the Criminology Society.

Chapter Four

James led the way to the contestants, huddled on the competition area's far side. They all had an air of varying levels of discomfort. James waved his hand to get their attention.

"Attention ladies and gentlemen." He spoke to them in a faint effervescence.

"Is Mr Lane really dead?" Sara Ware asked immediately.

"I'm afraid so, Miss Ware," James held his hands gently in front of his body to keep the tense atmosphere surrounding the group to a minimum. He was about to continue when McClain piped up.

"So what's this mean for the rest of the competition, then?" Kent asked. "Will we be packing it in altogether?"

"A man is *dead* and you're concerned about the competition?" Tilmann questioned with a rather phoney sense of consideration. James could tell he was just trying to appear chivalrous, likely for the ladies' benefit. It's what James himself might do.

"Enough." James rubbed his eyes. "We will worry about the competition later. For right now, there is an investigation to be managed." He gestured to Daniels.

"This is Inspector Daniels. He'd like to ask you all a few questions."

"What? He think one of *us* done it?" Hammond asked.

"Only if one of you did." Daniels answered casually.

"Fairly certain he just wants to know if we saw anything." Sara added once again. Daniels adjusted his hat, pushing it back a bit to peer at all of the contestants.

"Particularly if anyone here saw anything leading up to when the accident took place." He specified. "Let's start from the beginning, now. I'd like to speak to you individually."

"We need to come to the station?" Jaqueline asked.

"Not necessary, I can conduct the preliminary interviews here. Come over by the tree, each of you." Daniels pointed to Tilmann. "You first, sir." The two went over by the tree in question, out of earshot of the others. "Right then. Name?"

"Michael Tilmann, clockmaker." He stated.

"What brings you to a blacksmithing competition if you make clocks?" Daniels asked.

"Well, the gears." He stipulated. "I joined the competition in hopes of broadening my skillset, as well as hoping the reward for winning would be substantial enough to invest into a business for myself."

"And did you see anything leading up to the explosion?" Daniels pushed.

"I was more focused on prepping my tools." He pulled a shining pair of tongs from his apron with shaky hands.

"How do you think I keep these things so bright and shining? *Loads* of maintenance."

"And nothing seemed out of the ordinary?" Daniels was curious as this fellow seemed too full of himself to be so attentive to his tools. Besides which, there was something off about those tongs.

"Only the explosion, sir." Tilmann sighed. "I seldom see such things building clockwork. Nothing much louder than a cuckoo, so what I need at the moment is a stiff drink."

"I can see how such a sudden thing can fray your nerves." The Inspector nodded. "I may have to ask a few follow-up questions in the near future, so I have to ask that you remain in Oxford."

"Don't worry, Inspector. I have *no* intention of abandoning the prospect of that prize." Tilmann gestured inquisitively, asking nonverbally if he was free to go. Daniels replied in kind and waved to James to send another of the contestants over to him. James guided over Sara Ware who approached with apprehension.

"Miss Ware, isn't it?" Daniels asked. She nodded with her head sunken. The Inspector cocked his head to see her eyes. "Doing alright?"

"Not really, Inspector." She clutched at her own arms. "I'm sorry. I'm used to injuries on this job but I've just... I've never seen something like this happen." It was clear to Daniels that she wasn't a stranger to this work since her hands were traditionally feminine yet rough and calloused from much hard work. The opposite of Mr

Tilmann whose hands were soft as a baby's bum. It was also very clear that this had affected the poor girl.

"Miss Ware, we can do this later if you need. Just let me know where I can find you to speak about the matter." Daniels removed his hat to ensure his sincerity.

"Thank you, Inspector. All of us are put up in a hostel up north." Sara explained. I believe I'll be there for the foreseeable... and can you let Mr Mondey know to come and see me as well?" Daniels raised an inquisitive brow. "Oh! No, no! I only mean I wish to speak to him about my position in this event. Besides, I already declined and he seems to be more interested in *another*." She chuckled lightly as they both looked at him flirting with Jaquelin Brush.

"Ugh." Daniels rubbed his eyes. "Right then, on your way, we'll talk later." He shooed her away, calling a constable to take her back to her lodgings. Daniels then turned his attention to James. "*Oi!*" James barely stirred as he gestured Emannuel to head over.

"Inspector." Emanuel greeted. "Hammond, Emanuel." They shook hands—an unsurprisingly firm shake that smarted Gabriel's fingers.

"Daniels," The Inspector flexed his hand subtly to work out the pain. "I don't suppose you've got any information for me, have you?"

"That posh toff ain't got nothing for you, eh?" Emanuel derided Tilmann, but something about the way Hammond said that made Daniels suspicious. "Fella don't seem like the type for this work, do he?"

"Says he's attempting to broaden his horizons." Daniels fed into the conversation to get more information. Emanuel chuckled deeply.

"That there lad don't seem like the type to know the meaning of a hard day's work. Not like you and me, eh?" He nudged the Inspector.

"Indeed. Speaking of work, I need to get mine done." Daniels tried to direct the conversation toward the accident. "Is there anything you can declare that may have led up to this?"

"Hmm." Emanuel stroked his chin, looking inquisitive, but something about his face seemed disingenuous... like he knew something but was not saying. Daniels saw this same face on smug little hoodlums who thought the coppers had nothing on them. "Sorry mate, but I only arrived soon enough to get me tools in order before the party started, if ya know what I mean."

"That so?" Daniels nodded. "Well if you *do* think of anything off the top of your head, please come to the station. I'll also be stopping by your lodgings, likely tomorrow, to talk to Miss Ware."

"I'll keep punchin', Inspector." Emanuel poked at his own head. "Meantimes, I gotta go talk to a mate of mine 'fore I head back."

Daniels watched with narrowed eyes as Emanual made his way to the front gate of the park, or so the Inspector assumed. Something about that man roused suspicion. He knew more than he was letting on but for now, Daniels had to focus on collecting statements.

This time he opted to just walk over and talk to the final two contestants together. It would break up the attempted dalliance with Jaquelin. He couldn't have this interfering with the investigation. Upon approach, Kent McClain was sitting by his forge a short distance from the two of them.

"Thank the Lord. I couldn't take another moment of them two's ogling." Kent stood up. "Inspector, I've been thinking, there's no way something should have gone wrong!"

"How do you figure?" Daniels queried.

"I have a habit of keeping an eye on my surroundings as well as my work," Kent explained. "I saw what *everyone* was doing and every step Jeff took was absolutely right! Bloke was meticulous as anything!" Kent showed off his burn scars. "Believe me, Inspector, I know what a mistake looks like."

"So to your knowledge, this may not have been an accident?" Daniels pressed, hoping this might unthread a few loose ends.

"No way in hell, Inspector." Kent shook his head fervently. "I think someone screwed 'round with his equipment." Daniels found this useful since now he had more than just an amateur hunch.

"So you claim this was sabotage, then?" The Inspector replied.

"Had to be."

"To your knowledge, did anyone arrive early to the event?" Daniels continued to prod for information. Kent has been the most helpful so far.

"I'm not sure, myself. I arrived to have a bite at one of the stands here and then walked over to my station. By then, everyone was already here." The scarred smith explained his movements. It was then that Jaqueline broke away from her little canoodle session with James.

"I know that Hammond left the lodgings early." She chimed in from across the green. This piqued Inspector Daniels's interest but he kept his poker face.

"According to Mr Hammond, he only arrived in time for prepping his workstation," Daniels explained. James could see there was an air of gambling in this conversation.

"Then that was an outright lie!" Jaqueline crossed her burly arms.

Daniels turned to the large woman, interested by her sudden addition. As he looked at her, she had a serious expression. There was an adamant feeling in her eyes, unlike everyone else the inspector had spoken to thus far.

"Sure about that, are you?" He asked.

"No, it's a fact. I don't sleep too good, y'see." Jaqueline explained. "So I do a good bit of reading in my leisure time. Hammond's room is right next to mine and I heard him up and about, leaving his room at about five o'clock this morning."

"Interesting." James chimed in. "I arrived at nine myself and you were all here at the time."

"So when did the rest of you arrive?" Daniels directed his question to both smiths.

"I walked into the park with Kent there 'round seven." Jaqueline specified.

"Yeah, us smithers keep pretty early hours to catch up on work and such; to say nothing of the amount of prep time we have." Kent expounded on Jaqueline's point.

"Hm." Daniels wanted to mull on this further. "I think that'll be all for now. As I've told the other contestants, I'll be in touch to make further inquiries." Daniels tipped his hat and the two smiths started to make their way in the same direction as the others. Jaqueline also gave James a suggestive wink which the tempting tippler reciprocated with a small wave. "*Ahem!*"

"God, you're worse than Amelia." Snapped James with a roll of his eyes. Speaking of his eyes, they rested on something that he needed to direct the inspector *away* from! "Perhaps it's time we move along from here, I'll buy you a drink!" James placed his arm around Daniels's shoulder attempting to lead him away.

"I'm on duty Mr Mondey. Plus I have more to cover, I need to see if any of the people in the park saw anything as well. On an unrelated note, Miss Ware wants to speak with you at your earliest-" Daniels tried to pull out of James's grip only to see the very thing the eccentric cavalier tried to avoid.

Across the park, beyond the cordon, both men spotted Essie and Cecil speaking with one of the park attendees. Daniels huffed and straightened his vest, simultaneously giving James a snide glare.

"Can't blame me for trying." He shrugged.

"*Stay.*" Daniels pointed at the ground in which James stood.

"In your dreams, Gabe." He followed tightly to the inspector, hoping that if he failed to get him to go easy on his friends, he could at least direct Daniels's wrath at himself.

While Essie finished speaking with the park patron, Cecil was busy winding his watch. He remained thoroughly uneasy by this whole course of action that Miss Cyrus insisted on taking, but listened intently to everything that was being said.

"Thank you for that information, sir, it's been most helpful." Essie bid the man.

"Not at all, missy." The fine but casually dressed man doffed his non-existent hat as he turned to leave and enjoy the candyfloss in his hand which had left residue all over his face.

"Is he gone?" Cecil asked.

"On his way. Why wouldn't you even look at him?" Essie questioned the butler as his back was to them the entire time.

"His tie was askew, and I've found that people don't fancy a stranger adjusting their outfits. In addition, the state of that sugary gunk all over his face was more than I could bear." Cecil shuddered. He scanned the area only to see the Inspector and James coming over, the former looking irritable. "And here comes the hurricane."

"Hm?" Essie followed Cecil's gaze and smiled. "Inspector Daniels!" She waved.

"What do you think you're doing Miss Cyrus?" Daniels huffed as he finished his approach.

"I'm glad you've come, Inspector. I think I have some information you'll find most titillating." She began.

"*You* are not an officer of the law, nor are *any* of your book club's members," Daniels stated, calm but intense as he gestured to all three of them.

"What the hell did *I* do?" James shrugged.

"All I need from the lot of you is to clear the area, alright?" Daniels began moving his hands in a shooing motion to insist that they all vacate.

"Very well," Essie stated, much to James's confusion and Cecil's relief. They all began to make their way out of the park until Essie spoke up one last time. "Although, you may not know about the suspicious figure people heard talking nearby."

"Damn it all." Cecil sighed.

"Wait!" Daniels spoke up with a grumble. He was already exasperated when they all turned about to face him again. "Fine. Tell me what you have." He groused. Essie bounced on her heels wearing a proud grin.

"According to the witness statements, many craftsmen here at the event were accosted by a man called Mr Spinner, who represents Majority Armes." Essie's eager demeanour became more serious, but you could still see the excitement in her eyes.

"They are, evidently, a weapons manufacturer here to poach some good workers for their factories," Cecil added.

"That's not a crime." Daniels was quickly starting to lose interest.

"Mr Wood might disagree," Essie digressed but her smile returned. "But what makes this mysterious figure so suspicious is while shooting the breeze with people, he made comments about the possibility of something going wrong with the show." Daniels raised his eyebrow.

"People *heard* this? This Spinner fellow *hinted* at a bit of sabotage?" The Inspector was open to this information now.

"It was more like he was disparaging the equipment. Insisting that there would be an accident." The short maid amended. "Some people were taken in by his professionalism, but the forges were built by Sander-Son's who work for Mr Wood."

"*Nobody* that works for Roland does anything fragmentary." Cecil added.

"Interesting. That *is* interesting." Said Inspector Daniels. "Any of the witnesses see where he went or hear where he's lodged?"

"No, but that last gentleman with the candyfloss stated that he'd been seen throwing something away in that bin." Essie pointed to a rubbish receptacle along the walking path beside one of the booths.

"Right, you lot please vacate, I'll look into this." Daniels insisted, a bit more politely this time.

"Will you at least let us know what you've found?" Essie pleaded.

"He'll have to tell me since it was my event, and I'll tell you." James smiled mischievously. Daniels narrowed his eyes at James.

"It doesn't go outside your Criminology Society. You understand me, you three?" He pointed at them all again. They nodded in acknowledgement.

Without another word, the three friends made their way out of the park, agreeing to all visit the hospital to check up on Professor Cole. Daniels, on the other hand, called over one of his officers to accompany him to the rubbish bin to see if they could find out what this mysterious Mr Spinner tossed out. Hopefully, something that could tell them where they could find this mysterious man for a few words.

"This the bin, Inspector?" The officer, Boggs by name, queried.

"The one that was pointed out to me. Let me see." Daniels looked inside. "Hm. Well, that wasn't hard."

"You found what was tossed?"

"Indeed, and out of everything I expected, this was not it." Daniels reached in and pulled out a rather nice felt hat, barely worn. He also pulled a fine double-breasted vest, followed closely by an expensive-looking dark coat. "Now why would a man, innocently working for a weapons company, toss his fineries in a rubbish bin?"

"Seems like the man may have been a bit looney." The officer chuckled as he took the items for the Inspector.

Daniels dug in the bin further, pulling out what appeared to be brushed hair. A toupee perhaps? Or a stage beard of some kind judging by the sticky glue-like substance on the ends.

"I doubt that. I rather think he didn't want to be identified by those who saw him." Daniels pondered.

The man that Essie was speaking to was wearing some rather nice clothes, but only the pants and a tie. Also, if he was right, then the sticky residue on his cheeks wasn't from his candyfloss. Something was feeling off here. This case wasn't going to be as simple as Daniels hoped it would be. Seems anything involving the Criminology Society is anything *but* simple.

Chapter Five

Cecil drove the Horch from the park with James and Essie in tow. Cecil was eager to get home, as always, but he too wanted to check on the Professor. James and Essie both rode in the back seat, shooting ideas off of one another as to the implications of what they'd learned at the park.

"What would a weapons company gain by sabotaging the event?" James queried.

"Maybe it's not about what the *company* gains at all." Essie expressed her ideas with suppressed excitement.

"Coming up on St Julian's, you two. Conclude conversations and prepare to enter." Cecil said, wanting the proverbial iron to cool so that Essie wouldn't run wild on this mystery like she did in the dance hall debacle or the Prometheus case.

"Right, pal." James opened the door before the car even came to a full stop, much to Cecil's infuriation.

"Yes, just step out of a moving vehicle," Cecil's sarcasm was blunt and unyielding as always. "No way for you to get caught under the wheels, fall and break your thick head open!" The irritable butler braked to a full stop, still mumbling to himself. James stifled his laughter as he rounded the back to Essie's side, opening the door for her.

"How do you put up with him?" He chuckled, helping Essie out of the car.

"He's not so bad when you don't deliberately upset him." She replied.

"There isn't much that *doesn't* upset him."

"You both realize that I am *not* hard of hearing, yes?" Cecil said with a slam of the driver's door. "Shall we?" He gestured to the hospital.

The trio entered the building, each of them straightening their outfits from the short ride. Upon approaching the front desk, James took the lead. The nurse at the counter was a middle-aged woman of little consequence, but she had a very welcoming disposition despite her hard-looking features. She had clearly seen a few hardships in the medical profession but was likely the type to have a complete index at her fingertips to tell them where to find their friend.

"Can I help you?" The receptionist asked.

"Yes, we're looking for a Spencer Cole, he was admitted for an emergency." James finished but before the woman could even check her admission cards a familiar voice could be heard.

"*Si vous ne reculez pas et ne me laissez pas voir mon mari, la prochaine personne à être patiente ici sera* vous!" That furious voice echoing through the halls could only belong to one person. Seems that the seasoned nurse was not going to be a necessity for them.

"Ah, never mind, we can find our own way now." stated James.

"We'd best hurry before the morgue begins to fill." Cecil stated as they all turned their direction to the stairs ahead.

The hospital was large but by no means massive, with its predominantly Baroque architecture. It was originally built as a convent but was made into a medical care facility during the war. The arched halls carried the raucous protestations of Amelia Cole across the entire building, drawing the attention of patients and faculty alike! It was difficult for the others to tell how close they were to their destination since it sounded equally as loud no matter where they were. Upon turning the next corner, they saw Mr Wood, Susan and Andrea holding back Mrs Cole from a poor shaking nurse.

"I-I'm sorry, Miss-" The nurse attempted to quell the frantic French woman before having a rectification snapped at her.

"*Missus!*" Amelia clenched her shaking hands into stressful fists. "As in, *his* missus!" She pointed a violent finger at the door.

"Apologies, but I c-couldn't understand you." The nurse was referring to the shouting in a foreign language. "The doctor will be with you momentarily if you would just be kind enough to wait."

"I will make this simple, *chère*. I want to see my husband *now!*" Andrea and Mr Wood pulled Amelia back.

"Please do excuse her," Mr Wood tried to alleviate the tension. "She's a bit protective of her husband, you understand."

"Amelia, look at me." Andrea directed Mrs Cole to face her. "Spencer's going to be fine, okay? There was no surgery, he's just getting a once-over by a doctor. Now breathe." She directed Amelia in the same breathing technique that she taught Susan when her solicitude got the better of her.

The three new arrivals joined the group trepidatiously, trying not to upset the newly acquired balance. Susan was first to take notice of them, but before she could say a word the hospital room door opened. All eyes were upon it, ready to barrage the doctor with queries on their injured friend. To everyone's surprise and relief stood Spencer Cole, followed closely behind the doctor.

"*Mon amour!*" shouted Amelia.

"Ah, you must be the frantic wife disrupting the entire wing." The doctor sighed in an amused fashion. "I must say, you must be the most caring wife I've ever seen here.

Many women demand I *keep* their husbands rather than return them." He laughed.

"Is everything alright, Spence?" James asked from around Mr Wood.

"As it can be. I lost consciousness due to the shock of the explosion more so than the explosion itself." Spencer rubbed one of the scorches on his lapel. "Other than that, I'm relatively unharmed."

"That's quite the comfort." said Susan. "I think we'd all best adjourn to the outside of the building."

"For the comfort of my other patients, I think that would be best." The doctor indicated for the Criminology Society to leave, which they obliged.

The Society members all left the hospital much more calmly than Mrs Cole's arrival. She was fussing over Spencer the entire way out of the building. Upon reaching the car park, they all congregated near the Horche.

"Shall we all convene at Everjust?" Mr Wood bid the group.

"I'm actually still a bit shaken up from my experience." Professor Cole stated. "If it's all the same to you lot, I'd like to cocoon myself into my, um," He cleared his throat. "'*comfort zone*' for a while."

"Understandable." Mr Wood nodded. "You two go home and get some rest. Essie can fill the rest of us in on what I'm sure she's found." He nodded to her and she sheepishly nodded back.

"How did you-" She started to ask.

"You came in with James who I assume was still there talking to the police, meaning you stayed at the park. There is only one reason you would stay that I can think of." Mr Wood chided her.

"Too right," Said Andrea. "Being the world's best meddling maid, present company included." She pointed at herself.

Amelia gave the key to her car to Spencer for him to go and wait inside. The headstrong director stepped up to Mr Wood with that adamant expression she wore when conveying her intent.

"You find out who did this." She stated. "You find out who killed that man and hurt my husband and you make them pay for it." Mr Wood took Amelia's hand and patted it.

"We will, Amelia. You have my word." He assured her with all his being before she separated from the group to join her husband in the car.

There was little else to be said amongst the group until they returned to Everjust. Mr Wood accompanied James, Essie and Cecil in the Horche while Susan and Andrea took their own vehicle to drive across town to Holywell Street. To each of the members, the drive seemed to take forever as they were all itching to know what Miss Cyrus had in her head to share with the rest of the proverbial class.

Upon arriving at Everjust the Society entered the house. The surroundings took a load off of everyone's shoulders once they were in the familiar comfort of the entryway.

"Sakes alive!" Cook came barreling from the kitchen and hugged Essie while resting her hand on Mr Wood's arm. "I heard what happened at the park, luvs! I'm so glad you're all upright and on your feet."

"For the most part, anyway." Replied Mr Wood. "We'll be needing some refreshments if you please."

"Oh, aye! I'll fetch something from the top shelf, sir." Cook agreed. "Will the others be staying for dinner?" She asked, knowing she would be preparing for James. Susan and Andrea looked at one another. They had only just had lunch at the park and the situation they had just experienced certainly did not aid in having an appetite.

"I don't believe we'll be staying for dinner, but thank you." Susan spoke up.

"Righto, then." Cook went back to the kitchen to fetch the refreshments while the others convened in the lounge.

The room was quiet while everyone took a seat except for Mr Blackbird and Miss Cyrus. Mr Wood sat in his favourite chair across from the two ladies while Cecil waited by the open doors to the lounge. James lolled in one of the other seats in the room with his legs over one of the arms as he rested his elbow on the other. Cecil gave him an aggravated side-eye while James smirked at him impishly.

"So Essie, James, regale us with what you've discovered." Mr Wood stroked his beard, eager to know, as well as, to quell Mr Blackbird's wrath.

"Well, we learned that the executive from Majority Armes, a Mr Spinner, has been going around trying to snatch up talented metalworkers." Essie began. It was just as Mr Wood suspected, but not very damning to the murder. However, what Essie was about to say next would interest him much more! "He was also going around stating that he *expected* something to go wrong during the showcase today."

"Hmm." A deep hum escaped Mr Wood's throat with a slight growl in his voice. His eyes were wide having learned this. "Now that *is* interesting."

"Don't get too excited, Wood," said James, interjecting his point. "We also learned that one of my contestants, Hammond, lied about when he left the inn that they're lodged at. And something still irks me about Tilmann."

"Perhaps it's because he has a sense of class." Cecil mumbled, still irritated at James's skewed way of sitting.

"More like a sense of social climbing," James replied. "I think I don't like him because he reminds me of the people in my family." He sneered a bit. Essie's mind perked with several questions, being reminded of her American friend's family.

"Which reminds me, James, what is this business with your sister?" She asked, hoping it was still within the realm of the topic. James immediately flopped over the arm of the chair, his head hanging as he let out a loud groan.

"*Please*, I would rather discuss the prospects of a violent murderer over a cup of coffee than utter another word about that spoiled brat." He huffed. "She's going to have a field day writing to father about this."

"Do you suppose that's why she disappeared so suddenly?" Essie wrung her hands together as everyone felt that moment of clarity. James's head popped back up as he looked at her.

"Pardon?" He raised his sharp angular brow. Everyone's eyes darted to one another as they realized that the moment the explosion had occurred, Elsbeth Mondey was *nowhere* to be seen.

"Surely you don't mean to say that his sister is a suspect." Susan placed her hand on her chest in surprise.

"Don't get me wrong," James finally sat up properly in the chair, not that Cecil took notice as he was pouring drinks for everyone when Cook brought the bottle. "I would *love* to see most of my family in the hoosgow, but Elsbeth is neither ambitious nor is she intelligent enough to be behind something like this. She, like most of my family, takes pleasure in people's misery, but she would never resort to murder."

"Agreed." Mr Wood nodded as he took a glass from Cecil. "The motive is too minor for his sister. Money is important to the Mondeys but sabotaging James's share in his allowance would hardly guarantee her getting any of it." James nodded back in agreement, knowing it would likely just go toward more investments for his mother and father's own extravagance.

"Hang about though!" Andrea decided to chime in. "What if she never intended someone to die? What if she just wanted to muck up the show and make James look bad but it got out of hand?"

"Again, not smart *or* ambitious enough," James replied. "I am ruling Elsbeth out, and I think *I* would be the leading expert on that particular matter."

"Alright, alright," said Andrea as she held her hands up defensively.

"Mr Hammond lying about his whereabouts is intriguing." Mr Wood continued to smooth his whiskers in thought. "He sprung into action awfully quick after the explosion occurred. Not what one would expect from a cold-blooded killer."

"Unless *that* was by design," Susan added. "An attempt to look like a hero in front of a crowd?"

"Not enough data to support that fact, I'm afraid, Miss Jordaine." Cecil interjected as he handed the ladies a pair of drinking glasses. "I do agree that Hammond is the most important focus at this point in the investigation as we also haven't got enough on the mysterious Mr Spinner."

"Leave that part to me." Mr Wood stood up. "I have a few calls to make, Cecil. Keep our guests comfortable and make sure I have no outside disturbances." Cecil bowed at the waist as he took the now-empty glass from Mr Wood.

The prodigious master of the house took his leave of the lounge to head upstairs, but not before whispering something to Mr Blackbird which he nodded in response to. While they were unsure of what he'd said to Cecil, everyone knew that he was likely going to call in more than a few contacts to find out more about the elusive Mr Spinner. Finding this information before Inspector Daniels was also likely to hack him off, but he would welcome the assistance, surely. Essie hoped so, anyway. She leaned against Mr Wood's chair, unsure of what to do with herself now.

"Essie, dear?" Susan walked over to the pint-and-a-half-sized maid. "You seem out of sorts."

"I just wish I could do more." Miss Cyrus held her head high, but her eyes conveyed a dourness unbecoming of the usually sprightly maid.

"Come off it, Essie!" exclaimed Andrea. She sprung up in response to her equal's sour self-deprecation. "If you think for one second you didn't do enough, take it from me, Mr Wood would not be up there in his office following up on what you've provided!"

"Andrea's right, darling. I highly doubt the police would even have thought to look in the direction of this man if you hadn't gone above and beyond to find out more." Susan patted Essie's hand before taking her furtive paramour's. "Never doubt what you can do, you *more* than proved it the last time this kind of thing occurred."

"Thank you, madames." Essie nodded, reassured of her worth.

"Our pleasure. Now I believe I need to be heading home." Susan's expression betrayed a kind of exhaustion that she'd displayed many times before. "All this excitement has begun to catch up with me."

"I'll help you to the car, love." Andrea took Susan's arm and Cecil accompanied them to the front door.

Essie seemed to be doing much better until she saw the pensive look on James's face as he sprawled out across his chair again. He was staring at the moulded ceiling in what almost looked like a trance. It couldn't be the alcohol, he only had a single cup thus far, although he was more than likely to have Susan's untouched drink if it came to his attention. She'd sat it down on the side table shortly after it had been given to her.

"Mr Mondey?" She tapped his shoulder. He blinked and glanced over.

"Sorry, what?" James came back to reality from whatever universe he was travelling in. He glanced at his empty glass and held it up. "Oh, uh, could I trouble you for a top-up?"

"Not at all, sir." Essie smiled. James might have called her out on calling him 'sir' when, despite being in distinctly different classes, they were much closer than that, but he could see something in her.

"What's wrapping up *your* mind, Essie?" He asked her while she poured him another drink.

"I could ask you the same, *O Oracle of Ethanol*." She chuckled, as she chided him. Her sense of humour returning made James feel more at ease, but he also began laughing loudly at her joke.

"Ha! I should have that put on an identification card!" James continued laughing boisterously as he took the glass. "Ah, but really. Something seems off."

"Hm." Essie's shoulders raised defensively as she wasn't sure what was bothering her any more than James was. "I really couldn't say. Miss Susan's words were a great comfort, but something is still weighing on my mind." She relaxed a moment but remained uncomfortable.

"Believe it or not, I get it." James winked at her. "You're restless. It's like something under your skin is itching at you from the inside and it won't be satisfied until you do the thing you truly want." Essie looked at him, surprised.

"T-that's it exactly!" She sputtered. "How did you know?"

"I feel that all the time when I get bored. Personally, my issue gets solved by going out on the town and drowning myself in multiple forms of debauchery," He paused. "But somehow I doubt that would be helpful to you."

"It is most certainly better help for *you*." Essie agreed with a chuckle.

"You're like Mr Wood. You require a sense of progress," said James. "Tell you what, I intend to find what lavish gemstone my sister has opted to hide under. If I do, how would you fancy joining me in digging answers out of her?" Essie cocked her head to the side.

"But I thought you didn't suspect her." She was a little confused now.

"Of the murder, no. I do however think she's up to some mischief." James stood up and walked over to pour another one for himself, but finally spotted the abandoned glass beside the sofa. He crossed the room to claim it while still holding the empty glass in his free hand. "The longer I linger on the subject, the more I *do* wonder why she disappeared so suddenly after the explosion."

"Well," Essie pondered for a moment. "While I'm not sure it will scratch the specific itch I'm looking for, I suppose that it could be very edifying to know what Miss Elsbeth is up to."

James knocked back the drink and sat both glasses on the end table to empty his palms.

"It's a date then!" James and Essie shook hands.

Unbeknownst to them, Cecil was still in the hall. He was listening in on the entire conversation and he was worried. Essie was giving off that air that she had when she stood in front of a gun, desperately demanding answers. Or worse yet, when she snuck out of the house to put herself in harm's way on Mr Wood's behalf. Cecil was going to need to keep a tight eye on her for her own sake.

Chapter Six

The following day, Inspector Daniels sat in his office, filling out the necessary paperwork on this case so far. His next order of business was to find the hostel that the contestants were staying at. He had already spoken with Miss Clubb at her hotel, as it would have been inappropriate for a judge to lodge with the contestants. Unfortunately, just as he was getting ready to break away from his desk, in came Chief Inspector Blofeld.

"Gabriel, my boy!" Blofeld chortled. "What can you tell me about this incident at the park?"

"A possible act of sabotage led to a death during the blacksmithing competition." Daniels described the information rather abruptly, hoping Blofeld would realize that he was trying to continue the investigation.

"I see, I see." The tall man nodded with his snipe nose in the air. "I trust you'll treat this case with due diligence." He pursed his lips. "I received a call, you see, from a Miss Mondey." Daniels raised his brow.

"You mean, *Mr* Mondey, surely." He queried.

"No, my man." said the Chief Inspector, shaking his head. "Miss Mondey insisted that we close down the park until we can close this case."

"I don't think that would be necessary, Chief Inspector." Daniels could already see where this was going.

"Well, the Mondey family is a very influential group in the United States. I believe it would be best not to upset them." Blofeld nodded with a condescending tone.

"This lady Mondey, though, is not affiliated with the exposition at the park. *James* Mondey is," explained Daniels. "His is the only authorization I can accept. Plus, many local businesses are counting on the boost this event is giving them. Mr Roland Wood thinks so, too. He has a stake in this expo as well." Dropping more than one prominent name would garner Blofeld's opportunistic attention. "In short, you wouldn't want to upset the community, *plus* the elites who stand behind it, would you?" Blofeld's expression changed to one of poorly masked worry.

"As I think about it, it truly *would* be a shame to lock down the entire park." He began backpeddling. "And we've already placed a guarded cordon on the crime scene, have we not?"

"We have, sir." Daniels nodded. It was becoming easier to play Blofeld as he was weak to the will of prominence. It would someday prove problematic for carrying out law and order, but today the Inspector played his boss like a fiddle. "Now if you'll excuse me, sir."

"Where are you off to, Gabriel?" asked Blofeld.

"I'm on my way to complete my interviews with the contestants of the blacksmithing competition." He said passively, brushing off his superior.

Daniels had several irons in the fire at the moment. On the one hand, he had someone checking for explosive materials on the damaged crucible. He also had someone trying to track down Mr Spinner, the executive from Majority Armes, who for some reason decided to throw away an expensive suit and wore a false beard to conceal his identity. However, the most interesting thing pressing on his mind was the blatant falsifications that Emanuel Hammond had given him. Daniels was most interested in learning why the man would lie.

"Boggs! You're with me!" Daniels ordered a constable to accompany him. "We're on our way to the inn, north of the park."

"Right, Inspector!" The constable followed, as ordered.

They both hopped into a black and white and made their way to the location they sought.

Inspector Daniels was behind the wheel, leaving the constable to idle in the passenger's seat. He began looking through his notebook filled with what he'd taken down so far on the case.

"Sir? Why are we going to a hostel?" Boggs queried.

"I want to interview Mr Hammond again. According to one of the other contestants, he lied in his testimony." Daniels explained as they drove.

"About?"

"His whereabouts before arriving at the event. According to Miss Brush, Hammond had left in the early morning hours, yet he claimed to have left and arrived at the same time as the other contestants." Daniels listed the facts as they stood.

"Perhaps he went to breakfast?" Boggs shrugged.

Daniels shook his head, pursing his lips.

"Something feels off. One thing you need to do as an investigator is trust your instincts, Boggs. Working by the book at every turn leaves too many loose ends." The uniformed man looked to his superior. Boggs was a couple of years Daniels's senior, but he was beginning to understand why this young man made Inspector so quickly.

Meanwhile, at Everjust, the members of the household had finished their breakfast. Cook had prepared a lovely sausage and egg feast with toast and jam. Mr Wood had left rather abruptly without saying much and James was currently getting dressed to go out himself. Essie was already waiting for him in the foyer wearing a nice coat over her uniform. When the two convened, James put out his arm for Miss Cyrus to take.

"M'lady?" He smirked. Essie giggled and took his arm while he opened the door. They were both startled to see Mr Blackbird on the other side! Essie yelped, not expecting to see her technical superior standing there. "Good God, man! Why are you lurking on the front stoop!?"

"Where are the two of you off to?" Cecil inquired rather coldly, even for him.

"Oh, I've asked for Essie's help to have a few words with my dear sister. I think I've narrowed down where she'd be staying and I intend to ask more than a few impertinent questions. Afterwards, the Inspector said that one of the ladies from the contest wished to speak with me." James smiled with a snide tone as he discussed Elsbeth again, but upon mentioning the ladies at the inn, he became quite chipper. "So if you'll just excuse us." He started to walk through the door, but Mr Blackbird held out his arm to block them.

"You may do as you please, but Miss Cyrus is staying here. Under a *strict* watch." Cecil was still conveying himself in a harsh and impersonal way.

"What?" Essie's face sank. She felt a mix of confusion and outrage.

"It's for your own good, my dear." Cecil sighed, knowing this would make her very unhappy. "Frankly, I'm concerned about your wellbeing."

"My *wellbeing?*" She asked sharply.

"When these things happen you take too many risks. It's for your own safety, Essie. You need to be protected from yourself."

"*I'd* be with her." James tried to advocate for the small but powerful maid.

"I, and both of the Coles, were with her in the museum when she stared down the barrel of a gun for the sole purpose of having answers." Cecil sneered at James. "The last time I saw desperation like that, *you* were sober for almost an hour. Unless you can guarantee she won't pull a stunt like that, I intend to keep her here."

"Don't talk about me as though I'm not standing right in front of you!" Essie snapped as she squared up to Mr Blackbird.

"Please, Miss Cyrus-"

"Don't '*Miss Cyrus*' me! I am not a child for you to keep an eye on!" She grew ever more agitated.

"True." Cecil would live to regret his next words. "You are an *employee* for me to keep an eye on." He wore a stern look on his face. Essie's sank further to an expression of sadness. Her shoulders were stiff and tears welled up in her eyes.

"And yet I thought..." Essie didn't finish her statement as she turned her back and retreated up the stairs. James watched as the girl sequestered herself in her room. He looked to the stoic butler as his face also melted into a sombre visage of regret.

"You know, Cec, that is quite possibly the single *dumbest* thing I've ever seen you do." Which was saying something. James glared at him.

"It had to be done." His shoulders actually began to droop, messing with his normally perfect posture. "She will get over it once she receives whatever information you bring back."

"I'm not talking about what you *did*, I'm talking about what you *said*." James rubbed his left temple.

"I stated the facts. It worked did it not?" He gestured to the upper landing.

"You really have no idea, have you?" The American inebriate rolled his eyes. "If you know what's good for you, you'll prostrate yourself and confess to her."

"Confess?" Cecil seemed genuinely confused. "What have I to confess to Miss Cyrus?" James narrowed his eyes as he walked around Cecil.

"It's amazing." He nodded. "A perfect form of mechanical craftsmanship. You look human, you sound human, but bottom line, you still lack an understanding of human emotion." James abruptly left, leaving the remorseful butler to be offended by his comparison. "I'm taking the Horch, by the way!" He shouted. Cecil didn't reply as he was still processing what James had said to him.

With that, we return to Inspector Daniels and Constable Boggs as they approach the large cottage-style house that was the current lodgings of the blacksmith contestants. They opened the gate and approached along the cobblestone path. There were hedges lining the walkway, leading into the garden to the side. Opening the front door they could see a quaint little entryway into the dining room but before that was a desk next to a door that read '*Owner*'. The door opened and a sweet-looking little old woman stepped out.

"Good day, ma'am." Daniels tipped his hat. "I'm-"

"Dashed out of luck for a room." The old woman snapped. "I'm full up at the moment and I *don't* rent to *coppers*." She glared through her ridiculously thick glasses at Constable Boggs.

"Um," The officers shared a glance. "We aren't here for a room, ma'am. I am Inspector Daniels, Thames Valley Police, and I wanted to talk to your tenants about the accident that occurred in the park earlier the previous day." Daniels explained to the temperamental woman.

"Lovely, *now* I'm taking in tenants that bring coppers to the doorstep!" The lady sneered as she walked back to her room, grumbling the entire way. "Last time I take a bulk rent from a lousy Yank. Never did see the like, I tell you..."

"Charming woman." Boggs whispered, too afraid to test the landlady's hearing.

"Indeed." Daniels peeked over the desk at the registration book. He flipped the page and found '*E Ham &—?*' scrawled in the book. The other contestants' names were equally mis-spelled. "I don't think you had to whisper, Boggs." He stifled a chuckle as the woman was clearly hard of hearing based on these notes. The men walked through the dining room, taking note of someone's tool-belt hanging over one of the chairs, and up the stairs in the conjoining hallway. They went straight to the room that had been assigned to Hammond and gave the door a knock. "Mr Hammond? Oxford Police, we have a few more questions for you." They waited, but no answer.

"Oh, Inspector?" The officers turned to one of the rooms down the hall. It was Sara Ware. "I'm afraid Emanuel isn't in. He said he was going for some lunch."

"The lady doesn't provide one?" Boggs queried.

"She *does*," Miss Ware shrugged. "But I wouldn't call it gourmet... or prompt for that matter."

"Ah, I see." Boggs's curiosity was satisfied.

"Well, in his absence, could we finish talking to you?" Daniels gave a slight courtesy bow to the lady. She invited them into her room. It was small but lovely as it had a bed, a dresser, and a joint washroom. the white walls and unpainted wood framing matched the rest of the building's interior but tied everything together quite nicely. "So then, how are you holding up?"

"I'm doing considerably better than yesterday," Sara said, taking a seat on the side of the bed after pulling out a chair for Inspector Daniels. He obliged and took the seat while Boggs pulled his notebook back out. "Did you relay my message to Mr Mondey?"

"I did." He nodded. "Now, onto my questions; Can you tell me anything about Mr Hammond's comings and goings lately?"

"Emanuel?" Sara pondered for a moment, equally confused as to why Inspector Daniels seemed to be *so* interested in Hammond. "I'm afraid I'm not much help there, Inspector. I've been rather focused on my own itinerary of late. Couple that with the emotions that have been drowning me since the accident... it *was* just an accident, yes?"

"We have to keep all of our options open, dear." Daniels reached over and patted her shoulder. "I'm glad to see that you seem better, and don't fret, we'll get to the bottom of this. Knowing James Mondey, you'll be fine to stay here."

"Actually, I believe a man called '*Wood*' is footing the bill." This caught Daniels's attention. Why would Mr Wood be paying for anything while James is equally wealthy?

"Why's Mr Wood doing a thing for this event?" He knew they were friends, but this kind of thing is no small chunk of change, even for a rich man.

"Well I don't know how true it is, but I've heard through the grapevine that Mr Mondey hosted the entire event because he's been threatened with a cutoff." Seems Sara knew more helpful information than even *she* thought.

"That's interesting." Daniels gestured to Boggs to write down that information.

A knock at the door drew everyone's attention. Daniels stood up and walked across the wooden floor to the door. Upon opening it, he saw James Mondey!

"Someone's ears were burning." Daniels smirked.

"Inspector! Good to see you. Is Sara in?" He looked over the policeman's shoulder, giving the small smith a wave.

"Before you go in there, I'd like to ask you something." Daniels closed the door and the three of them, Boggs included, walked down the hall to Hammond's door. "Is it true that you're hosting this whole thing so you don't get cut off?" James blinked with a stunned grin on his face.

"How in the second circle of Hell do you know about *that?*" James asked bobbing his head sharply on every syllable!

"I see. And you didn't think this was pertinent information?" Daniels crossed his arms trying to keep his voice low. The constable jotted this new revelation in his notebook.

"Not really. I barely knew the guy. Why would someone kill Jefferey to get to *me?*"

"I think it could have less to do with you and more to do with your money." Daniels was thinking about the call that Blofeld had taken earlier that day. "Do you know a *Miss* Mondey?" James rolled his eyes so hard that his head moved along with them.

"Not you too. I told the others and I'll tell you, Elsbeth is not behind this!" Daniels shushed James and popped the brim of his hat.

"Elsbeth, eh?"

"My horrid sister. And far more useless than me, which, believe me, is no small feat." Daniels was thrown off by the wash of negatives that James just shoved his way. The Inspector's confused silence gave James an opening to take notice of the door they were standing by. "This Hammond's room?"

"Uh, yes. He's not in, though." Daniels rubbed his temple.

"Ah, good." James tested the knob, noticing the door was unlocked.

"Mr Mondey, you can't do that." Daniels grabbed James's arm.

"Correction, *you* can't do this without a warrant." James began counting on his fingers. "I am the benefactor of his show and, therefore, welcome at any time. You, not knowing this, see a suspicious figure entering a suspect's room and are professionally obligated to go inside and search for anything untoward." He shrugged as he entered the room. Daniels huffed in aggravation and followed him.

"One of these days I'm going to walk into the station and find out that you're in one of the holding cells, aren't I?" The Inspector's sarcasm was well-received with a laugh from James.

"Honestly, it wouldn't be the first time." James was sifting through the drawers in the nightstand. He whistled a sprightly tune while Daniels stood hand to mouth, trying to keep his emotions steady. "Hang on, what have we here?" James pulled a small vial of powder that was wrapped up in a dirty bit of cloth.

"What's that?" asked Boggs.

"If I knew that I wouldn't have said '*what have we here*'." James cocked his brow with an amused smile. He then dropped it from his hand, which Inspector Daniels practically dove to catch! "*Oops*, the suspicious figure seems to have dropped something that should be tested in a chemical lab."

"Mondey, you should be a lawyer." Daniels sneered, trying to mask his interest.

"Have a *job?*" James feigned disgust. "An *influential* one that would actually give me something to *lose* if I pursued my favourite pastimes?" He stuck his nose in the air in an exaggerated way. Boggs tried to suppress his laughter.

Daniels pocketed the vial and was about to chastise James further when they were all startled by a scream from outside! Without another word or thought, all three men ran down the stairs and out the front door.

"Around the side!" Daniels led the way, gaining his bearings from their position in the house.

They all followed the short path to the garden and rounded the corner of the house. The scream had come from a woman in a fine dress. James recognized her immediately.

"Elsbeth!?" James shouted angrily. "What are you doing here!?"

"Forget about that, James!" Elsbeth pointed them over to the rosebushes, unable to verbalize her intent. Daniels ran over while Boggs and James stayed with the frantic debutante. The Inspector carefully pushed some of the bush to the side.

"What do we have, Inspector?" James shouted to him.

"One less suspect." Daniels huffed. "It's Emanuel Hammond. He's dead."

Chapter Seven

The old bird that ran the inn was a ranting mess with the officers who arrived on the scene. She had to be confined inside since she began bopping one of the bobbies with her cane for stepping on the petunias. Despite the crowd of investigators outside, they could still hear the woman shouting and stamping her cane on the floor from inside the house. It was almost amusing.

All of the remaining contestants were gathered by the front door in a tizzy because of the grim commotion. They had already been told by James that Hammond had been found dead in the garden. All of Sara's improvement was suddenly undone. She looked like Susan when she was about to have one of her attacks.

"Mr Mondey, I'm afraid I won't be able to continue in this expo of yours!" She cried. "This is too much."

"It's okay, Sara." James gently put his hand on her shoulders to calm her. "Just stay until this ordeal is over and we'll discuss things when the case is closed. Okay?"

"I don't know." She whispered.

"We might as well, luv." Jaqueline leaned over beside her. "We can't leave till the case is over anyway, and the competition is on hold I'd think, too."

"True. We can't continue the exposition with you lot while the investigation is being handled." James shrugged. "Even then, I'm not so sure about continuing with it so long as the rest of the event is a hit."

"Cancel the competition?" Tilmann piped up. "I took time off work for this! Room and board isn't money in my pocket, mate!"

"Agreed!" Kent snapped. "Every day my shop's closed is a day I'm out commissions!"

James was surprised by the outrage but also felt completely stupid that he hadn't considered everything they'd put on hold for this. McClain is a one-man shop as it is, so it would be remiss of him to just toss the competition aside.

"Okay, I take your point." James sighed. "We'll discuss things further down the road after this whole mess is resolved. Alright?" This seemed to quell the group. Someone *else* seemed to be enjoying this misfortune, though.

Elsbeth had already given her statement to the police and used up her crocodile tears. That girl had never had a realistic cry in her life, even when she was afraid. She was hiding a smirk as she glanced at her brother. James made his way over to her with a sneer.

"*So* is the demoness enjoying her meal?" He gave a sarcastic smirk before staring hard at her.

"What?" She was genuinely confused but was still entertained by his frustration.

"Well you *do* still feed on the misfortune and agony of others, don't you?" James narrowed his eyes as she grinned snidely. "What are you even doing here? I stopped by the Randolph and they said you'd be visiting this inn. Now I *know* you aren't shopping around for a different room and it's not a coincidence that you came to the place that my contestants are staying." She shrugged callously.

"Can't I take an interest in a family event?" Elsbeth continued to smile at him in a condescending way.

"No." James angled his brow. "The only contribution *you* could offer the family is to marry a wealthy guy."

"My, my, and I thought you were the *progressive* one." She feigned outrage. "To think, you have such an opinion of women."

"Not women, just you." James folded his arms. "My assurance that you're a useless little brat is the only reason you aren't a suspect in this." Elsbeth's mouth dropped open.

"*Me!?*" She snapped.

"Miss Mondey, I presume?" Inspector Daniels interjected. Elsbeth adjusted her demeanour of haughty arrogance and smiled at the Inspector.

"I am. How may I help you? I've already spoken to your strapping officer." She gave a fake wave to the cop who interviewed her.

"I understand you called my superiors and said you were planning on closing down the entire event?"

"You *what?*" James was outraged but kept his composure. Elsbeth twitched her brow smugly and gave her brother a cocky half-shrug.

"No worries, Mr Mondey. The cordon only extends to the forges." Daniels allayed James's concerns before refocusing on Elsbeth again. "Back to you, Miss. I wonder why you decided to interfere in your brother's work if you have no stake in it. It might shed some light on why you came here at an *oddly* inopportune time."

"I'm sorry, are you accusing me of something, Officer?" Elsbeth sneered once again.

"Inspector. And that depends entirely on your answer." Daniels remained stern and unwavering. A person's money was not intimidating to him, even if it was to his boss.

"Well, I'll have you know, that I am here on behalf of the Mondey family." She explained with her nose in the air. "Dear James, here, doesn't offer an abundance of confidence with our father. I was asked to make sure that my brother does not bring *more* shame onto the family name."

"How noble of you." Daniels rolled his eyes and turned to James. "Say the word and we'll see to it that she doesn't come anywhere near you or your people."

"No worries, she's a petty annoyance. No danger." James shook his head. Elbeth stamped her foot, her dainty shoe making a loud clack against the stepping stones!

"We'll see about that, brother dear. I wonder how Father will look on your event now that it's on hold because of a murder." She grinned at James with her hands on her hips. Her handbag dangled on her arm rather heavily. This confused James as all she usually had in there was a chequebook and some face powder.

"Nice try, but even Father can't find fault with *me* over something like this." James was right. Much like he'd been teased about earlier, James was a genius in finding loopholes and the Mondeys are honour-bound to their word; which is why most of their shameful dealings are carefully cultivated. James can fight fire with fire.

"We'll see... We shall see." Elsbeth turned her back and walked away.

"I didn't dismiss you Miss Mondey!" Daniels snapped at her. She only gave a princess wave in response. "Do *not* leave Oxford until this is over, madam!"

"Wouldn't miss the results for the world, Mr Daniels!" Elsbeth crooned as she walked down the street.

Daniels and James watched as she disappeared down the street, likely to get into a car she had waiting. James was thoroughly annoyed but the Inspector's blood had come to a full boil. He hated dealing with rich people... present company excluded.

"Infuriating, isn't she?" James chuckled, amused by the rage that he could see Daniels hiding.

"How did you grow up with that?" He asked earnestly.

"Immersion. My family is like taking a dip in icy waters." Daniels was confused by James's weird comparison. James noticed and laughed. "I mean, the longer you stay in the more you're used to it, even though it is still unpleasant." *Now* he understood. "So what do we know?"

"Hammond? Cause of death was clearly a blow to the head." He directed James's attention to the garden. "The side of his head was totally indented. Possibly a hammer."

"Someone did in *Hammond* with a *hammer?*" James queried as they both walked toward the house.

"Tasteful as always." Inspector Daniels shuddered, keeping his emotions under control.

Both men entered the inn. James followed the Inspector as he seemed to know exactly where he was going. Daniels went into the dining room and pulled out a handkerchief from his pocket to pick up the toolbag that he had seen in there earlier. Upon searching, he took an inventory of the tools within. They definitely belonged to one of the blacksmiths, and just as he thought, the only tool that was missing was a hammer.

"What are we thinking?" James asked over his shoulder.

"I'm thinking that the murder weapon came from this tool belt," Daniels replied. "Considering there doesn't seem to be a hammer in here. I should have everyone take an inventory of the contestants' tools, just to be sure."

"Well, I know who to start with. These are Tilmann's tools, for sure." James took the handkerchief and picked up a chisel bit. "Look at this thing, it's immaculate. Barely even looks used *and* it's polished." He was right. These tools were shiny and looked brand new.

"Tilmann? That's something to go on." Daniels picked up the belt and slipped over behind the front desk again.

All of the contestants returned to their rooms on the orders of the police, leaving Daniels having to search the records again. To say nothing of having to decipher the crazy old landlady's misinformed coding system. He found Tilmann's number and proceeded to seek the young man's door to knock on. Conveniently, Tilmann's room was directly next door to Hammond's.

"Mr Tilmann? It's Inspector Daniels." He said as he knocked on the wooden door. "I have a few questions for you." The door opened with a slight squeak.

"Inspector? How can I help?" Tilmann opened the door and invited Daniels in.

"First and foremost, can you explain this?" Daniels raised the toolbelt in his hand. If Tilmann was masking his surprise, he was doing very well at it because he didn't seem taken aback at all.

"My tools?" He shrugged.

"There seems to be an important piece missing from it. Care to take inventory?" The Inspector held the belt in front of his face. Tilmann took it and poured the tools out on his bed. He scratched the back of his head and shrugged again. "The hammer seems to be missing."

"Yes, yes, you're right!" Tilmann pointed his index over every tool and was very put out to realize that the hammer was *indeed* missing!

"The victim, Mr Hammond, had his head stoved in. And your hammer is missing."

"Now wait a minute! I left my tools unattended wherever the hell you found them." Tilmann defended himself, finally starting to seem worried. "Anyone in this place could've stolen my hammer and killed Emanuel! On top of that, my old dad gave me that hammer so as soon as you find it, I want it back!"

"Well, Mr Tilmann, I'm afraid if we do find it it's going to be evidence in our murder investigation." Daniels could see why James didn't like this man. He seemed more concerned with his stolen tool than the fact that it was used to kill a man!

"Then once you figure out who has it, arrest them, hang them, *clean* the thing and give it back! Until then, go and find who *actually* killed Hammond instead of making speculations!" Tilmann stamped his foot as he demanded that the Inspector leave.

James could hear the raised voices as he entered Miss Brush's room, at her behest. On one hand, he couldn't wait to be in the bed chambers of the gorgeous Amazon of a woman but he also wanted so badly to eavesdrop on the raised voices... being in a room with a strong woman won out in the end.

"Seems Tilmann is gettin' riled up." Jaqueline raised her brow.

"Yes, it turns out that Hammond may have been killed with his hammer. He's likely peeved that the good Inspector is grilling him." James adjusted his tie. "So, were we convening to make some dinner plans or some such?"

"Nice as that sounds, Luv, I actually wanted to talk to you about Tilmann." Jaqueline sat on her bed to be just under eye level with James.

"About the murder?"

"No, actually." She was a bit sheepish about the subject as this seemed like very small news compared to the second murder in this event. "I think Tilmann is a fraud. Take his tools for example. I had a look at those things, and they're brand new! He doesn't maintain them meticulously, they're fresh from a hardware store! On top of that, a few of his tools aren't even the right *kind* for blacksmiths!" James nodded, acknowledging the information this woman was giving him. In his mind, it was starting to make sense why he didn't like that man. He was a liar! "That's not all, either. There ain't a professional metalworker alive who'd just leave their tools about like that. *Not even* a clockmaker."

"What are you saying?" James didn't quite get that little tidbit. Likely because he wasn't making *eye contact* with Jaqueline at the time.

"Do you know what he turned in for his entry?" Jaqueline questioned him.

"Hmm. I'm afraid for the sake of keeping the competition alive I shouldn't mention-"

"You haven't a clue, have you?"

"No. The judges are well aware, though. I can find out from them." James started to walk to the door. "Can't thank you enough for all you've given me to think about. How about that dinner to pay you back?"

"Oh, you *are* a smooth operator." She commented on James's prowess as she bit her lip suggestively.

"I can also operate *rough*, should you prefer." James purred as he slowly closed the door behind him.

James took a deep breath and turned away from the door, attempting to vent his excitement to conquer that mountain of a woman. He tugged at his collar as he opened his eyes to see Daniels standing in front of him, arms folded.

"*Oh, god almighty!*" James nearly fell over by the Inspector's sudden appearance. "Don't *do* that, it's already unnerving when Cec does it!"

"Can you please not go trying to stir up my investigation with your '*little spoon*'?" Daniels grabbed James by the arm and they both went back downstairs.

"First off, it's more of a '*serving spoon*'," Daniels growled in disgust and smacked James in the shoulder. "Ow. And secondly, what do we have on Tilmann?"

"Not much, I rather fear. The fact is, he left his tools in the open, meaning *anyone* at the inn could have taken the hammer and struck Hammond dead." Inspector Daniels shook his head with aggravation. "I'm not so sure I can count him out, but I don't have anything else to suspect him with."

"Well, Inspector, if you give me some time, I just gathered some intelligence that may clear things up for both of us one way or the other." James had a plan, which the Inspector didn't dare ask. No euphemisms were running through his mind, however, as the person whom he intended to talk to was the judge he was closest to. Spencer Cole!

Meanwhile, at Everjust, Cecil was obsessively polishing the clock in the foyer. He had been doing that for nearly half an hour, glancing up toward Essie's room every so often. He was wracked with guilt over how he treated her, but he knew that a firm hand was the only way to keep the overzealous maid safe. This was an odd feeling for Cecil since he never regretted a thing in his life, least of all how he spoke to anyone. Why was Essie so different? It didn't make sense in his mind.

Cecil was stirred from his thoughts by a swat on his shoulder with a ladle!

"*Ah!*" Cecil groaned as he took notice of the fact that there was now some sort of sauce all over his shoulder. "Cook! Why did you do that!?"

"Mostly, 'cos of what you did to that poor girlie. Also 'cos you've been standing there ignoring me." The stout woman waved the utensil at him. "You ought to be ashamed of yourself, Cecil Blackbird." Cook fixed her hands to her hips as she looked up at the perturbed butler.

"I am!" He shouted, trying desperately to brush off his shoulder. "I just wish I understood why. I've *never* felt guilty about enforcing rules or speaking bluntly before. Why now!?"

"Oh, you stupid boy." Cook shook her head, which drove Cecil up the wall!

"That's what Mondey said! What are you people on about!?" Cecil threw down his polishing cloth.

"Well, don't tell him, Cook." Mr Wood called down from the upper landing. He had returned from his previous errands and was preparing to head out to follow up on more leads soon. "He'll figure it out for himself eventually."

"Roland. What have you found?" Cecil queried, trying to ignore his anger at everybody over keeping his own feelings a secret from him!

"Still inconclusive. Have my coat and hat ready, I'll be heading out shortly to follow up on my findings." Mr Wood requested as he crossed the second floor. "In the meantime, I'll try putting in a good word for you. And Cook? Some tea, please?" He requested, pointing at Essie's door.

Both domestics agreed and set out to work while Mr Wood tentatively approached Essie's bedroom door. He knocked on the door gently. No answer. He knocked again, slightly more firm.

"Whoever it is, I'm not really in the mood to talk." Essie's small voice crept through the door.

"Then I suppose I'll have to pull rank, won't I?" Mr Wood slowly opened the door and poked his head in with a small smile.

Essie was at her vanity desk and stood up when Mr Wood came in. She tried her hardest to hide the fact that she had been crying earlier.

"I'm sorry, Mr Wood." She sniffled.

"Those tears because of Cecil?" He pointed to her puffy eyes.

"I... it's nothing." She folded her hands on her apron.

"It's not his fault. Don't feel too harshly toward the poor dumb lad." Mr Wood sat on the side of the bed and patted it. Essie followed the clear instructions and sat next to him. "I was the one who told him to keep you here." Essie looked at Mr Wood, a mixed expression on her face. "I'm worried about how much you've been putting yourself into dangerous situations. I wanted to make sure you don't go doing that again, at least until I had a moment to talk to you about it."

"I'm just trying to help." Essie replied, choking back more tears.

"I know, Essie, but the last thing anyone in the Criminology Society would want is for you to get hurt." Mr Wood placed his hand on her shoulder. "Now, look at me, child. I care a lot about you, and what you have been doing goes beyond just a need to feel useful."

"What are you implying, Mr Wood?"

"I'm afraid that the night we spent in the Jilde Estate has had a lasting impact on you." He stated. "I think you crave closure. Think about it, please. If things hadn't transpired the way they had, would you still stare down a gun demanding the '*whys*' behind a crime?" Essie opened her mouth but no answer came out. She hung her head, almost contemplating the answer herself. "I just want you to think about your safety more often. Don't take too many risks... at least no more than me. I'm the veteran between us."

"Well, don't take this the wrong way, Mr Wood, but you are also much older now too." She held back a chuckle and Mr Wood laughed much louder.

"I suppose you're right." He laughed again. "But all the same, I'd rather know *you're* going to be safe. And I'll make sure Cecil apologizes. I told him to keep you here, I didn't tell him to break your heart." Essie sighed with a smile.

"My heart's not really broken. He did what he did because he cares, just like you. I just wish he could be a bit less brusque about it." She stated.

"Yes, well, you and me both. Don't let him off easy, though." Mr Wood patted her knee. "Make him stew for a bit. The poor twit doesn't even know why he feels guilty about the situation and I'd like him to learn the hard way. He doesn't understand '*emotions*'."

Essie tilted her head, eager to accept Mr Wood's instructions but equally confused about why he wanted Cecil to suffer those consequences. Probably to make him learn better manners or figure out his '*emotions*'. Whatever the case, Mr Wood stood back up and walked over to the door.

"I hope you'll still stay here for the time being until I come back with more information." He requested.

"Well, I do still have some housework to catch up on. I've sulked enough." Essie nodded as she got up to clean her face.

"Don't bother with the foyer clock. It's been polished to within an inch of its life." Mr Wood exited the room and made his way to the front door where Cecil was standing with a hat and coat in hand. "Alright there, Cec?" He was clicking his tongue similar to a clock and barely listening to his employer. Not that he listens much anyway. Mr Wood had to pull the hat and coat from the butler's grip.

"Oh, sorry." He stated.

"Apologize to the girl." Mr Wood put on his hat and walked out the door. He was still unaware that James had borrowed the Horch, but that would change. He was currently in a better position to afford a cab than his young American friend. It was probably about time to get a second vehicle. He wasn't very fond of the prospect of being one of those wealthy people who own an impractical amount of cars, but if this was going to be a pattern, then a second car might be very practical, indeed.

"What?" Cecil tilted his expression. He shook his head and looked up at Essie's door once more. This time she was standing up, leaning over the bannister and looking down at him!

Cecil was startled and tried to shuffle into one of the nearby rooms, bumping into the wall as he did so. Essie giggled as she watched him retreat and Cook walked into the foyer, hands once again on her hips as she shook her head.

Both women were stirred from their amusement at Cecil's befuddlement by a ringing. The house phone behind the stairs was echoing into the house. Essie hurried down the stairs, excusing herself past Cook to reach it before the person on the other end hung up. She spun around the corner and snatched the receiver.

"Wood residence." She said, attempting to control her breathing after the rush.

"Essie?" Andrea's voice came from the other end of the call. "Good, you lot are home."

"Well, Mr Wood only just went out, to where I don't know," Essie interjected.

"Bollocks. I was hoping to catch Mr Wood to accompany me." She explained. "I thought of an old, uh, '*friend*' of mine that sells fireworks. If I'm right, then he may be able to tell us if anyone bought anything that makes a bigger boom than a sparkler."

"Hm," Essie smirked a bit. "Well I suppose *I* could step out to offer you a hand-"

"*Over my dead body!*" Cecil's voice boomed from both another line on the phone and from the lounge.

"I knew you'd be listening, Cecil." Essie's grin grew as the dead silence of his embarrassment was deafening until a sudden click harmed both ladies' ears.

"He sounds more tightly wound than usual." Andrea's voice dripped with a cheery cynicism.

"He made me cry earlier and can't figure out why he feels bad," Essie explained with a giggle.

"... He's going to be the next body to drop." Andrea growled.

"Leave him be, I'm in the process of convincing him to be your guide to this questionable firework merchant of yours." Essie craned her neck around the corner to see Cecil's face. "You'll go with Miss Karras, won't you?" He stood there silently, avoiding eye contact with pink cheeks. Cecil nodded sheepishly. "Good, he'll be ready."

"Thanks for that, Essie. I'll come pick him up."

After hanging up, Essie folded her arms and looked at Cecil, who was still standing at the corner of the hall. He straightened his back but was still a bit twitchy.

"So," He cleared his throat. "I'll be off then. Please, don't leave."

"Oh, *now* you ask politely." Essie managed to keep a straight face as Cecil went rigid and his eyes rolled around like a pair of dice.

Cecil opened his mouth but wisely opted to turn around and retrieve his coat and hat. He put on his bowler hat and pushed it low as he ran through the front door. Cook once again shook her head as she looked over to the petite maid.

"Keep up the good work, luv." She smirked.

Chapter Eight

James Mondey came to a stop outside of the Coles' residence. He exited the Horch and smoothed his hair in the reflection of the window before strolling up to the front door and giving a rhythmic knock. He waited patiently with a smile on his face because he knew that the longer it took them to answer, the more entertaining this was likely to be. James looked at the watch on his wrist and chuckled to himself.

"Once my funds are reinstated, I should get a new watch. Gold plated with a diamond inlay." He was talking to himself to pass the time. It entertained him to think of all the ways he could get back to using his family's money to hurt them.

The latches on the door began rattling. James looked to see a very dishevelled Amelia Cole peeking through the crack in the door.

"James, *espèce de connard*, what are you doing here so early in the morning?" She groaned. James looked at his watch once again with a confused squint.

"It's well after noon, *mon ami.*" replied James. He raised his wrist and showed her his watch. Amelia blinked, surprised.

"Ah. In that case, come in." She backed away from the door, allowing her friend to walk in. James sealed the door behind him and checked the windows for the shades. "*Ne t'inquiète pas*, James, we *never* open the windows." Amelia waved her finger at James as she rubbed her eyes with her free hand.

"Sounds to me like a dismal way to live, but I suppose I understand several reasons why for you two shut-ins." James winked at her.

"Which reminds me," Amelia craned her neck to the staircase. "*Chéri! James est là, rendez-vous partiellement présentable!*"

"*Oui mon amour!*" The Professor's voice trilled from upstairs.

Amelia shuffled into the cluttered sitting room across from their kitchen, moving several archaic books off of one of the chairs and proceeded to flop into it with her legs crossed. James smirked at the messy hair and unkempt dress clothes that Amelia was adorned in. She noticed and narrowed her eyes at him, conveying him to keep his mouth shut. James was seldom the type to follow such orders, vocal or otherwise.

"I see you've been giving Spencer some very *special* medicine." James winked again with his emphasis. Amelia held her index finger up, aimed directly at his chin.

"Be nice, *mon amour*." said the Professor as he entered the room with his normally mussed sandy hair finger-combed and immaculate makeup on his face. It was unusual for facial cosmetics to remain that nice, but James was also slightly disappointed to see Spencer wrapped in a robe. "Good morrow, James. How are things in the investigation?"

"That's exactly what I've come for, actually," James smirked as he looked between the couple. "You were the one who reviewed the entries for each of the contestants, yes?" Spencer nodded.

"Why do you wish to know that?" Amelia queried, searching the desk for one of her cigars.

"I put them all upstairs, darling, you know how I feel about you smoking near the artefacts," Spencer added before realigning his attention to James. "Now what about the entries?"

"I want to know who entered what. *Particularly* what Tilmann entered." Spencer had a look of acknowledgement.

"Funny you should ask. I began thinking about the things I'd seen before the explosion knocked me off my feet." Spencer put his hands together under his chin. A telltale sign he was deep in thought. "Tilmann's entry was a very intricate letter stamp with his own monogram. Originally, I thought it made sense because of his work with clocks, but I remembered something from the competition." James was intrigued.

"Oh?" He pressed. "Don't keep me in suspense, old friend."

"Well, it was the *way* he was working during the competition. He wasn't moving with much urgency... in fact, he was more preoccupied with what the other contestants were doing." Spencer was illustrating Tilmann's movements, including looking over his shoulder while making hand gestures like he was handling the tools.

"Was he even working at all?" Asked James.

"I passed his station twice and he didn't even have any alloys in his forge. He was still just polishing his tools and..." Spencer squinted, placing himself behind the eyes of Tilmann. "He took his apron off and placed something in a small nook under his station. I remember seeing that out of the corner of my eye, but I was too focused on going to the next forge which ultimately crushed me under the weight of the Mara." James and Amelia both stared at him, cluelessly. Spencer sighed with a roll of his eyes. "A Germanic dream demon that causes terrors, it's where we get the term *nightmare*."

"Could you not just say you were knocked unconscious?" James shook his head, frustrated. He then froze and practically lept into Spencer's face. "Wait! You just said that you saw him place something under his forge?"

"Indubitably. I remember everything from just before the explosion like I'm staring at the portrait that brought me and my wife together." The pair entwined their fingers.

"Well, that's so sweet I'm about to need some heavy dentistry." James rolled his entire head before making his way back to the front door once again. "Thanks for the help, and if you two should ever need the favour returned, my offer still stands to spice up your-"

"Happily monogamous, James!" They both snapped simultaneously, prompting James to run out of the house, laughing, followed by a wingtip striking the door behind him.

James chuckled as he nodded innocently to the nearby municipal tree trimmer. James ignored the no-account stranger and hopped into his borrowed car. Maybe it was time to invest in a new vehicle that, this time, wouldn't disappear into the night with one of his dalliances.

James drove to the park in the Horch and tried to get his bearings. The park was disappointingly devoid of many goers. If he didn't hurry and solve this case, his event was going to dry up, as would his funds. He hurried over to the competition area only to see the worst possible sight he could imagine.

Elsbeth Mondey was behind the cordon, which infuriated James. How many more times was he going to be subjected to the horrible visage of his sister!? And why did the officers on guard let her in!?

"Hey!" James shouted. Elsbeth looked up and smirked haughtily at him with a coy wave. "Stop her!" James ordered one of the officers. Two of the guards kept her from leaving while he charged up.

"Mr Mondey, I-"

"Hold that thought. Why did you let her through?" James asked.

"Uh, Miss Mondey is your sister, yes?" He nodded in an angered confirmation. "She told us that you'd sent her to pick something up for the Inspector."

"*That* is a bald-faced lie." James rounded the officer and approached Elsbeth. "Out with it you little cow!" Elsbeth huffed and slapped her brother across the face. The officers attempted to restrain her but James waved them off. "Ease up, this isn't unusual for her."

"*You* are the most *boorish* piece of dung on this earth!" Elsbeth tugged away from the officers that surrounded her.

"Have you any insults that you didn't use when we were small children?" James sneered at her as he scanned her. His arched brow lowered when he noticed that she was holding her arm rather stiffly as though she had something hidden under her coat.

There was something wrapped in a cloth sticking out of her coat. Before Elsbeth could argue with him any further, he reached for the corner of the package with exact precision and pulled it from her coat. The two of them were always stealing from one another, even when they were small.

"Give that back, James!" She tried to snatch back the folded cloth, dropping her handbag in the process.

The surrounding officers couldn't figure out what to do at this point. The pair were tormenting one another like overgrown children! James was waving the package above his head, keeping it out of Elsbeth's reach. Their shameless bickering was devolving into utter ridiculousness, fraught with petty insults and reminders of past transgressions!

As the officers looked on in perplexed amusement, Inspector Daniels arrived at the park to take another look at the crime scene. He came running when he noticed the discord unfolding within his destination.

"What the hell's going on here!?" Daniels smacked the officers' shoulders. "Separate those two, you idiots!"

The officers sprung into action and stepped between the siblings. James backed away with the folded apron in hand while Elsbeth continued to try and reach him from behind the arms of the officers.

"*Miss Mondey!* You're interfering with a *criminal investigation!* If you don't leave this *moment*, I'm placing *you* under arrest!" Daniels yelled at her at the top of his lungs, making her back away. Even James was taken aback by his rage. "And you! Give that over! It's evidence!" James obliged and handed Daniels the folded apron.

James leaned in as Daniels unfolded the apron to find a brick of some sort of metal and a small well of brass paint. Neither man was an expert in metallurgy, but it definitely wasn't the alloy that was provided for the competition!

"Where was this?" Daniels asked.

"According to Professor Cole, Tilmann was seen stashing this under his station. Further proof is that this is his apron." James patted the fabric.

"Oh, is it now?" Daniels was intrigued.

One of the officers cried out in pain and collapsed to the ground. Both men turned their attention to the distressed sound and he was holding his knee on the ground with Miss Mondey standing over him with her handbag dangling in her fist.

"That's what you get for shoving a *lady*." Elsbeth turned her nose up.

"I've had enough! Cuff her, now!" Daniels roared as he stormed over. James had to hold back his laughter at the thought of his ill-tempered sister getting arrested in a foreign country. "Get up, mate." Daniels ordered the officer on the ground.

"Agh, my leg's been knackered, Inspector!" The officer groaned as he tried to stagger back to his feet.

"For goodness sake, Officer, it's only a-" Daniels trailed off as he took the handbag from Elsbeth. Her face went pale upon the Inspector doing so. "What the blazes have you got in here, woman?"

"Nothing! Now give that back, it's my private property!" She stamped her feet as she was detained by one of the officers.

"It's what you used to harm an officer of the law, ma'am. And it feels like you've put a rock in here." Daniels shoved the bag into one of the officers' hands. "Put her in the back of my car. She's getting one of our finest criminal suites for the night." Elsbeth tried to wring herself free as she was dragged away kicking and screaming. "Sorry about this, James."

"I'm not." James chuckled. He held up the items they'd taken from her. "I realize this stuff is evidence, but I wonder if I might persuade you to allow me to have some of my own experts have a go at these? They'll likely get it done quicker than your lab fellows."

"Hm... I shouldn't, but I could always argue that the chief wanted it done quickly." Daniels shook his head. "As it stands, I'm still waiting on the analysis of that powder we found at the inn."

"Well, Manhattan wasn't built in a day." replied James.

"Rome, you mean."

"You have *your* standards, I have mine." Daniels rubbed his eyes.

"Don't make me regret this, Mr Mondey. You can pick up your sister tomorrow morning if you please." He stated. "Make sure nothing happens to those supplies or it's *my* head on the chopping block."

"Relax. According to Mr Wood, Blofeld's a blowhard who will turn a blind eye to anything that gives him favour with the upper crust." James shrugged as he rewrapped the metal brick and paint bottle in the apron and held it under his arm. "If you need me, I'll be returning to Everjust."

"Alright. Tah." Daniels tipped his hat as he turned to return to his car.

James rushed himself to the Horch. He could have spared a few minutes, easily... That's actually a lie. James Mondey is, to this day, one of the most restless and impatient men on the face of the earth. It is a trait that more than half of the Criminology Society shares. His mind was already racing with thoughts revolving around the revelations that have transpired today. James was nearly sober as a judge, which was impeding his ability to think on his usually advanced level. He needed to rush down the rapids of his crashing thoughts to find the answers, but alas he was trapped in still waters, proverbially speaking. If he had a pint of alcohol, he'd have probably noticed something that would save him a considerable amount of trouble later.

Meanwhile, across town, Andrea Karras was weaving through the light traffic with Cecil clinging to the seat. It amused her, given that it reminded her of her mistress's apprehension when the street-wise retainer was behind the wheel.

"Did you not notice that road sign!?" Cecil screamed as his free hand which didn't have a grip on his seat was clutching his fob watch. "It means to *stop* for traffic!"

"There was no one on the street, we were fine." Andrea chuckled.

THE CRIMINAL'S CRUCIBLE ~ 113

"*Watch the pedestrians!*"

"We're far from the sidewalk! Calm down, you."

"You're driving like a *maniac*, woman!" Cecil's immac- ulate hair had long since become a tousled part. "The very next homicide is *likely* to be caused by *you!* And I will tell you right now, I *will* throw you directly under the- *bus!*"

Andrea pulled the car back into its own lane of traffic as they'd nearly clipped the front end of a town bus. The horn blared as they whizzed by.

"You're worse than Susan. At least my dear mistress can keep her complaints to a minimum." Andre laughed at his expense once again.

"That's probably because she's *petrified in this seat!*" Cecil continued his inane screaming. "*Where* are you even taking us, besides potentially to the *afterlife!?*"

"I happened to think of a fellow I once knew who sells fireworks." They rounded the corner as they got further and further toward the outside of Oxford's city limits.

"Are you planning a celebration!?"

"Not exactly. You see, he's got a few questionable con- nections to the Galleanists in America and some under- ground followers in London." Andrea spoke so casually about this subject.

"Anarchists!? How the hell do you know a man who has connections to anarchists!?" Cecil knocked his fist against the door.

"He makes *really* fine fireworks." Andrea flashed a coy smile.

"You really *are* out of your mind, Karras! Is that why you wanted *me* as your companion and not your surreptitious paramour? To keep her away from the unscrupulous types we're going to meet?" Cecil continued to point at all the violations that Andrea was committing on their little jaunt.

"Exactly. And I'm hardly going there on my own. I'm still a lady, after all." She made an affectionate pose as she drove.

"Hands on the wheel!" Cecil growled once more before they came to a halt on a street corner. The uptight butler was hyperventilating as he started winding his watch to calm himself.

"When you're finished, could I trouble you to get out of the car?" Andrea stood alongside his door, tapping her foot. Cecil merely glared at her as he removed himself from the car, moving stiffly like one of the small mechanical figures that pops out of an artisinal clock. He slammed the door behind him.

"This was payback for my tone with Miss Cyrus, wasn't it?" Cecil attempted to smooth his hair back once again.

"No, mate. That's my normal driving." Andrea scowled at him, not liking the critique of her motorism. "Payback for making Essie cry will be a lot more painful and loads less subtle. Now, come on." She tugged on his sleeve as he proceeded to polish his timepiece to oblivion. "You're a complete burke, you know that, yeah?"

"I suppose you're going to be completely cryptic as to why, like everyone else in my life right now." Cecil groaned.

"Well, you're not going to learn your lesson if someone just tells you the answer." Andrea shook her head as they both approached an alleyway between two buildings.

The pathway was every bit as seedy as Cecil had expected. He half awaited someone with a small knife to pop out at any moment, but that was a jaded idea in his mind. On the other hand, Andrea clearly wanted an able-bodied gentleman on hand just in case something untoward started occurring. This may not be London, but unsavoury types exist everywhere that civilized society does. It's enough to make one question the definition of the word '*civilized*'.

The pair entered a shop that was situated in the basement of one of the commercial addresses. Inside the room, there were numerous exciting fireworks the like of which Oxford sees in the skies for special celebrations. As Cecil looked at the amazing things, he couldn't help but wonder if they were even in the right place. Everything looked very festive.

Andrea walked up to the front desk and rang the bell. There was no reply from anywhere in the shop. She rang it again.

"Oi! Freddie! I know you're in there!" She cried out. A tumbling sound came from the adjoining room behind the counter. Out came a man with thinning dark hair and an open-collar shirt draped over with a black powder-covered Tang suit jacket with pinstripe trousers held up by leather suspenders.

"Oh, Andrea." The man, Freddie, brushed off his oriental jacket. "Sorry, lass. 'Was afraid it was the peelers.'"

"And why would that be Mr... Freddie, is it?" Cecil looked at the suspicious Englishman down his nose.

"Who's the toff?" Freddie asked.

"My bodyguard," Andrea stated, leaning on the counter. "And you're lucky I'm the one knocking on your door right now."

"I'm well aware! That explosion at the park has jaws wagging all over town." He slapped his hand on the desk.

"And you're worried about someone official popping by to stick their nose into things you'd rather they don't, eh?" Andrea gave that sly grin she always does when she's looking to get something from someone.

"What is it you want, lady?" Freddie narrowed his eyes at her. "Because whatever it is, it'll come at a fancy price since I happen to know you've got some special sort of in with that employer of yours." He rubbed his fingers together. Andrea scowled and looked at Cecil, who raised a brow at the questionable shopkeep. He waved Andrea aside and stepped up to the counter, leaning over it ever so slightly.

"I believe we *can* cut a deal." Cecil spoke up, taking a glance at his watch before dangling it from its chain between his fingers. "Tell us what you know about the explosives, and we won't have our *dear friend* Inspector Gabriel Daniels know where they came from." Freddie's face turned pale while he tried to maintain a poker face, to no avail, and Andrea folded her arms with that smug expression. The owner shuffled in place, uneasy.

"I see your bodyguard is as ruthless as *you*." He lifted the counter and directed the two to follow him. "Not out here." He pulled the curtain shut behind them as they crossed into the back room he had come from.

The back room did not have the same festive charm as the shop itself. The back had several house-made fireworks in varying stages of completion, but there was also a great deal of equipment that looked far more nefarious than some celebratory pattern poppers.

"So it's true." Cecil sighed, tucking his watch away again. "You develop dangerous devices of destruction for dissidents." Freddie stared a moment.

"What the hell'd he just call me?" He asked Andrea.

"I told my friend here about your extracurriculars. That's why we're here." Andrea kept her arms folded. "If anyone acquired something highly explosive like what I saw that day, *you* were the one it came from." Freddie's expression was intense and worrisome.

"Aye, you're right. To be fair, I had no idea what his plans were for it, least of all that he was planning on using it locally." He shrugged.

"Who was he?" Cecil queried the man.

"When people ask for things like Cyclonite, they don't exactly sign the logbook, nor do I ask." Freddie huffed.

"Cyclonite?" Andrea finally unfolded her arms, intrigued.

"Cyclonite, RDX, whatever name you want to use for it. It's a solid crystal that the fellow asked to be shaved down into a finer substance. I gave him a few little vials of the stuff, one brick didn't go as far as I expected." Freddie explained.

"What did this bloke look like?" Cecil queried.

"Tall, brand new felt hat, fancy vest like yours, pricey dark coat. He had a shaggy beard, looking like some squared-away gigolo." This description was familiar on *two* counts. The description of the suit...

"His tie?" Cecil asked.

"What about his tie? What's it matter?" The shop-owner asked.

"Nice material but crooked?"

"Well... yes, actually. The knot was practically turned about." Freddie moved his hands around his collar to illustrate how mussed the tie was. Cecil was convinced now. He immediately left the back room to leave the shop. "What's got into him?"

"He does that," Andrea stated. "I'd recommend you head out of town for a while until this blows over. No pun intended." She followed Cecil, leaving Freddie to continue his frantic packing to prepare his temporary egress. Upon catching up to the high-strung butler she threw her hands up. "What was that about?"

"*I'm* driving this time." Cecil placed himself in the driver's seat, no arguments. "I need to tell Essie about something."

"Oh, you're finally going to confess to her?" Andrea smirked as she slid into the passenger seat.

"Confess? Why does everyone think I have something to confess to her!?" Cecil cocked his brow at her. She scoffed.

"Forget it. What are you on about, then?"

"The man that your Mr Freddie described was Mr Spinner of Majority Armes, I'm certain of it. And apparently, *we* spoke to him at the park the day of the accident." Cecil growled as he put the car in gear and pulled out much quicker than Andrea had expected. It was not nearly as mad-dashed as Andrea's driving but for Cecil Blackbird, it was shockingly reckless. He rounded one of the corners with a skid and all!

"Wow. This really has your goat." Andrea enjoyed the ride if only because it was entertaining to see Cecil lose his composure.

"I'm just desperate to tell Miss Cyrus." His resolute expression was practically intense enough to replace the headlights at nighttime.

"Why's that?"

"Because she'll want to know that the man we spoke to was actually Mr Spinner *and* that he was likely the one who purchased the explosives that killed Jefferey Lane."

"I got that, but why are you desperate to tell Essie instead of Inspector Daniels?" Andrea's question was met with dead silence and Cecil's face adopted an expression similar to that of a schoolboy taking a test he had not previously studied for. "Don't hurt yourself there, mate."

"Quiet."

The pair made it back to Everjust, where there was another car in front of the house. Cecil got out of the car and offered the driver's seat to Miss Karras. She was instead, desperate to aid in sharing the information with Essie. As they entered the front door, they could hear a discussion between Essie and James in the study.

"Oh! Mr Blackbird!" Essie called as she saw the pair enter. "Andrea, come in! There's been a dreadful development!"

"How dreadful are we talking?" Andrea crossed her fingers hopefully.

"Emanuel Hammond is dead. His head was clubbed in out in the garden." James illustrated a striking motion. "We think the weapon was Tilmann's hammer, as it seems to have gone missing."

"On top of that, according to James's latest conquest, Tilmann may have faked his way into the competition!" Essie pointed out. Andrea and Cecil looked to James, who pointed at the things he'd found beneath the forge sitting on the side table beside him.

"I've called Professor Cole to come and take a look at this. I have a sneaking suspicion that our man was planning to use a softer metal to mould his creation rather than forge it." James explained as he ran his finger across the metal brick. "Initially I didn't know what to make of it, but after getting home I managed to mull it over with a brandy."

"Or three." Cecil fanned his hand around James, inferring that he could smell the alcohol on him. "Well, we've found some hefty information ourselves."

"Yes indeedy." Andrea placed her hands on her hips. "Thanks to the more dubious side of this city, we know exactly who purchased the explosives used to blow the forge to bits." Essie was on the edge of her seat, clearly to all but himself that it sent Cecil's heart aflutter.

"Do you remember the gentleman that you spoke to at the park? The one with the crooked tie?" Cecil pointed at his much straighter neck adornment.

"Of course, that's the part you remember about the man." Essie shook her head, trying hard to hide her amused smirk. She was still intent on making Cecil feel her frigid glenohumeral joint on everybody's advice.

"Well, it would seem that he pulled a fast one by telling us about the VIP from Majority Armes." Cecil nodded to her. "In other words, he was telling us about *himself*." Essie sprung to her feet and James leaned forward with his angular eyebrow raised!

"What!?" Essie exclaimed. "You mean I actually *spoke* to him!?"

"And you'd be able to identify him if we ever find him. I think the Inspector will be quite eager to, as we also learned that he purchased several small vials of an explosive powder called Cyclonite." James slowly stood next to the butler.

"Small vials?" James asked. "The Inspector and I found a small vial of fine powder in a drawer in Hammond's room!"

"Well, this is all starting to come together quite interesting!" Andrea smiled. "I should ring up Susan and share these discoveries!"

As Andrea picked up the receiver to call up her double lover and mistress, the doorbell sounded. That was odd since everyone usually knocks instead. Cecil retreated to the foyer to answer the door, fully prepared to send a peddler on his way if that's who just interrupted their important business.

"Oh, Inspector." Cecil was surprised to see Daniels. Gabriel had a very solemn expression which piqued Cecil's curiosity as he invited the lawman in. "It seems we have a visitor, ladies and lush."

"Mr Mondey, I'm glad I caught you here." Daniels sighed.

"Where else would I be?" James chuckled. "Have a seat, I've called the Professor to tell us something about this chunk of metal that we've got here. But that's not all! It seems we have a new development as to who might be pulling the strings on this hectic investigation!"

"James." Daniels paused, trying to find a gentle way to put what he was about to say. "Your sister is being charged with murder."

The entire room fell silent as the grave. In the dead air, one could hear Susan Jordaine's voice calling for Andrea to respond as she was standing with her mouth agape.

"Pardon?" James asked with a slight tremble in the blinking of his eyes.

"Upon sticking your sister in a cell to cool her heels, we took a look inside of her bag. The reason she'd done so much damage to my officer's leg was because there was a blood-covered hammer wrapped in her own monogrammed handkerchief hidden within it."

James Mondey's head was reeling. Not because of some revelation that his sister killed a man, but that someone could even think that she was capable. Worst of all, that she could have put herself in a position that she could even be a suspect!

"That little idiot." James rubbed his forehead. "Gabe, you can't honestly think that she has something to do with this. There's no motive."

"I know, but I am unfortunately bound to follow what the evidence suggests," Daniels explained. "As it stands, I was rather afraid you would jump on this. There didn't seem to be any love lost between you and your sister."

"I don't give a damn about her. I'd be only too happy to see her locked up for something, but if she gets pinned with this, a killer goes free." James said with crossed arms. "I don't know why that stupid little tramp had that hammer, but I can assure you it's not because she *used* it!"

"I'm not entirely convinced either, but unless you have something to cast a reasonable doubt on this, I'm being pushed to charge her with it all for the sole reason of trying to sabotage her brother's accomplishment."

Daniels gestured to James. "You made it abundantly clear just how much animosity there is between you two."

"As it happens, Inspector, my dear friends Cec and Andie managed to find out something quite intriguing." James hung on Cecil's shoulder, to which the butler stepped aside to allow him to stumble over.

"It seems that the mysterious man from Majority Armes made a purchase of an explosive substance known as Cyclonite." Daniels listened to Mr Blackbird speak intently.

"Did I just hear you right? Our analysis people finally got back to me stating that Cyclonite was the substance in that vial we found in Hammond's room. There were also traces of detergent powder mixed into the bottle."

"Detergent powder?" asked Essie.

"Yes, apparently it is a practice used by some smiths to fortify their alloys and increase the heat around the metal. It also matched the explosive residue in the burst crucible." Daniels explained. "As near as we could ascertain, the explosives were poured onto the top layer of the container of detergent he was using." James clapped his hands together and held them out to Daniels.

"So he poured the powder into his crucible and the heat built up inside, resulting in the devastating explosion!" Essie completed the thought.

"Most of the damage was contained by the forge," James continued the thought. "but Lane got the full-focused blast..." He gave a small sigh of sadness before perking up. "So then, you can still continue investigating from here, right?" He exclaimed cheerfully. He was hoping that there was just enough reasonable doubt to keep the case open with so many outstanding pieces still floating around.

"Unfortunately that brings me to something else we found out, which I'm afraid might also implicate Miss Mondey." James groaned as he rolled his head and flopped over into the chair. "It seems Mr Wood has been hard at work himself, running hither and thither to find anything he could on Majority Armes."

"And?" Essie asked on behalf of James who was covering his entire head with his arms in frustration, twisting in the chair in an extremely childlike manner.

"It doesn't exist." Came the voice of Mr Wood from the foyer.

Chapter Nine

"What the hell do you mean '*it doesn't exist*'?" James had thrown his hands up in the air as he performed the air quotations with his digits.

"Just that, James." Mr Wood handed his coat to Essie, who had trotted up to take it for him. "I contacted every person I knew who might have some information on this company, or Mr Spinner. I even called in a couple of old favours—nothing. Not a single person or company has ever heard of Majority Armes weapons."

"So you're telling me that Mr Spinner was a fake? Perhaps trying to drum up business for himself?" James speculated based on Mr Wood's new discovery.

"I didn't say that it is some form of 'upcoming' company, I'm saying there are no records of any such company ever having been listed or licensed." Mr Wood went on. "Spinner is apparently using a fake company as a means to cover something up. Based on what James just told you, I'd say that he was covering his tracks for the purchase of an explosive."

"But he wouldn't have given his *name* for that." Cecil carefully pontificated, so as not to reveal that they'd spoken to the seller directly in front of the Inspector.

"True, but clearly he is falsifying himself left and right," Daniels added in. "And I'm afraid this wouldn't exonerate your sister, per se. As I was going to tell you, a claim could be made that he was under *her* orders. She does have that kind of money and influence after all."

"True, but Inspector, you can't tell me you're buying that." James clapped his hands together in synchronicity with his last few syllables.

"*I* do not. However, I'm illustrating exactly how the far more narrow-minded top brass will view things." Daniels shrugged. "I can try and push the idea that Mr Spinner is still a person of interest, but there's still the matter of that blasted hammer." James stood back up and placed his hands on the Inspector's shoulders.

"Two birds, one stone." He said. "I'm going with you to see my sister and get to the bottom of that. I also want to express my mock displeasure with your boss about this. If anything will stay the charges, pleasing a man with deep pockets should."

Daniels nodded his head, holding back a smirk. He was certain Elsbeth Mondey was hiding *something*, but he was unconvinced that she had anything to do with the murder. James was far more likely to get the information out of her than another officer. Mr Wood and Cecil's allegations toward the mysterious Mr Spinner had him spiralling further down the rabbit hole. How does he fit into all of this?

"Alright." The Inspector nodded again. "Come with me then. The rest of you..." He paused, hesitant to proceed with the statement. They all stood with bated breath. "I can't officially ask this of you, but please find out more on that walking red herring, Spinner. I want to find out why everything keeps trailing back to questions about him."

"We'll do just that Inspector." Mr Wood agreed with a bow of his head.

"Come on!" James called from the entry hall.

"Americans." Daniels scoffed as he followed James to the car.

As the two of them pulled away from Everjust, they left the rest of the Criminology Society to mull over how to hunt down this mysterious man. As obsessive as Essie Cyrus could be about these puzzles, Mr Wood was more desperate to uncover answers pertaining to the threat this so-called businessman may pose. If he *is* a representative of a weapons company, then that is as good as a threat of war in his opinion. But if he isn't a weapons representative... what could he be hiding that he wouldn't mind *that* being his cover?

Upon arriving at the station, James led the way into the building. Daniels tried to get him to hang back, but he was a man on a mission. James was ignoring the lawman's attempts to quell him as he approached the front desk.

"Elsbeth Mondey. Where?" He snapped.

"What?" The poor unsuspecting station clerk winged behind the desk. Daniels inelegantly shoved James aside.

"Log a visitor for Elsbeth Mondey, I'll escort him." Daniels snatched James's vest by the low v-shape and dragged him through the office to head into the holding area. "You must be the scrawniest runaway train I've ever met."

"I am neither a runaway train nor am I '*scrawny*'." There was an inuendous tone in the second half of that sentence, prompting Daniels to stop abruptly with his elbow extended outward for his companion to collide with. "*Oof!*"

"I truly wish you had an off switch." Daniels led James into a small room with a table and two chairs.

"Interrogation room, eh?" James entered and took a seat at the table.

"I figured you'd prefer a private moment with your sibling." Daniels remained in the doorway. "I also would rather not repeat the row the two of you had at my crime scene where you can disturb anyone. This is much more preferable." Daniels closed the door, leaving James to his thoughts.

As James sat alone in the dimly lit room, he felt more and more disdain for his sister and her foolish actions. Whatever she was doing with that hammer could only be something ridiculous to bother him. He ran through several scenarios in his mind as to how the conversation would go... none of them were pleasant. His thoughts swirled in his head, which should have been killing time, but instead, it was just like having conversations with his family over and over again. It was exhausting.

The handle to the door finally rattled, shaking James from his irritating thoughts. It was time to put his imagination to practical use. Daniels opened the door and he pushed Elsbeth into the room.

"Sister." James sat with his legs crossed and his chin balancing on the back of his hand.

"I suppose you're enjoying this, aren't you?" Elsbeth huffed as the door was locked behind her.

"Not as much as I would like. You being arrested would be greater than anything I could ever do to hurt the family, but the fact is, I can't have this." James straightened his position in the chair. "Have a seat." He pointed at the chair opposite him.

"I'll stand." She narrowed her eyes. "The smell of booze on you is bad enough from here." Elsbeth mocked him by wafting her hand.

"Fine, you stubborn brat." James stood up himself and squared up to Elsbeth. "Why did you have that hammer?" She remained silent, but her hardened demeanour seemed to falter. "I can only assume that you were there to find some way to sabotage my event in some way." She still remained very silent, but not out of defiance. She was searching for something to say that wouldn't be incriminating. Elsbeth knew full well that the police would be listening in.

"I found it." She stated.

"You 'found it' next to a dead body." James specified. He spoke with an angry curl in his lip. "Why would you do something so unimaginably and recklessly *stupid?*" Again, Elsbeth held her tongue. "*Elsbeth!* You are a whisker's width from being charged with *murder!* One that I know full well you *didn't* commit! Whatever you tell me couldn't possibly be any worse than that!" James shouted into her face. She was backed against the wall in shock as she'd never seen her brother this way before. They've fought, but this was him being more serious than she ever thought him capable of.

"I..." She sighed, still defensive as he back pressed against the plaster wall. "I intended to plant it somewhere to make things difficult for you." This time it was James's turn to be cryptically silent. Elsbeth watched as he held a mixed expression while staring a hole through her head.

"You were trying to incriminate *me?*" He asked.

"Or at the very least cause you some difficulty. I didn't expect them to actually suspect you, but I *did* expect there to be some questionable press that I could flaunt in front of Mother and Father." She tried to slide to the side and get around her brother, but he slammed his fist against the door next to her!

"You *tampered* with a crime scene and possibly altered our chances of finding a *killer* so you could *make me look bad!?*" His rage was boiling over. An extremely uncommon occurrence for the normally laid-back phi-landerer. "I have never struck a woman that didn't ex-pressly ask me to, but I am *dangerously close* to **beating** this selfish, careless, *disgusting need* for disparaging me to the detriment of others *right out of you!*" James con-tinued pounding his fist into the door, resisting the urge to aim it at Elsbeth! Instead, he grabbed the back of her neck and dragged her to the chair, shoving her into it. "This is not about my allowance anymore! This is about the lives of *two* men and possibly the safety of others! If you don't tell me what you know in earnest *you* are the one who is going to jail for murder! They are about to charge you!"

"What!?" Elsbeth was shocked. She was well aware that she was in trouble for striking an officer and for having the hammer in her possession, but in her sheltered mind there was no way that could implicate her!

"Yes, you little idiot!" James leaned down and contin-ued to shout in Elsbeth's face. "Did you really think that being a rich American meant you couldn't be implicated in this!?"

"Well, yes." She shrugged so nonchalantly, confused by what information could possibly contradict that logic.

Inspector Daniels and Constable Boggs were waiting outside of the room, watching from behind the tinted window. Daniels knew this was going to be an unfriendly conversation, but now he was regretting leaving James alone in there. Boggs was sure James was going to start beating the woman, but Daniels was hopeful that James could control his emotions.

"You had means, motive *and* opportunity based on everyone's testimony! I myself have said you would do almost anything to try and hurt my chances at this event running smoothly, but I also stuck my neck out and assured everyone that you lack the conviction to commit a murder!" James continued chastising her, slapping the back of his hand into his other palm. "And need I press on you once again that you were found with the *murder weapon in your possession!*"

Tears had long since welled up in Elsbeth Mondey's eyes. Solely for fear of her own well-being, but still, they were probably the first true tears James had ever seen her shed.

"I found it next to the big man!" She choked back a sob. "I'd come to the inn with the intention of bribing a few of them to leave Oxford altogether, but I heard arguing in the garden. I stayed behind the wall, I didn't see who was arguing with him." Her voice became a bit more serious as she tried to recall events as they happened. The truth was a relative concept to her, so she was in need of some hard thinking. "But I did hear a thump and a fall. I think the hammer was left behind by accident because I inadvertently broke a twig under my shoe and could hear someone running off."

"You said Hammond was arguing. What was it about?" James was no longer yelling this time. He was genuinely seeking information.

"He was blackmailing someone. The person who killed him said they wouldn't pay, but the large man said that he could prove that he was responsible for the explosion." She waved her hand about. "Then I heard that thump."

"Hm." James vocalized in acknowledgement, but he was so deep in thought. There was an obvious choice, but a common occurrence is that it's *never* the obvious choice.

"Do you really think I'll get arrested for this?" Elsbeth asked James.

"For murder? No. I fully intend to find the real killer, which will let you off of that." James continued thinking, not looking at Elsbeth as he pondered. "You're likely to have charges for tampering with evidence, but unfortunately, you're wealthy, so with our family's influence, you'll probably receive what's tantamount to a scolding and a dunce cap." He sneered. Elsbeth was relieved but picked up on the fact her brother was mad that she wouldn't receive the same punishment as an average person. "I'm going to go speak with the police now."

"How soon will I be released from this dismal place?" Elsbeth queried. James felt a spark of joy in that question due to the answer. He smirked, but quickly wore his poker face as he turned to face her.

"I'm afraid you'll be here until we find the true killer." James shrugged. "Can't release someone suspected of murder until proven otherwise." He clicked his tongue with an exaggerated shake of his head.

"Now wait just a minute!" Elsbeth shot out of her chair as she approached the slamming door.

James stifled a laugh to himself as Daniels and Boggs approached him. Boggs remained slightly behind the Inspector, nervous to approach the normally jovial young man.

"Hello, boys. Enjoy the show?" James rubbed his hands together.

"I sent you in because I knew you would get answers, but had I known you were going to be *that* rough, I'd have thought of something different." Daniels sighed. He was displeased with the display of violent screaming he'd just witnessed.

"She's never known a moment of serious suffering in her life." James merely straightened his vest as a show of his being unbothered by the inspector's protestations. "I'm done simply playing with her head. It's time she saw the definition of the word '*consequences*' in the real world."

Daniels still didn't favour the treatment of the girl, but he could hardly argue with James's logic. Not only that but to his credit it seemed to work. Elsbeth Mondey had refused to say anything to the police outside of a class-based insult that in her mind was a blow to their egos. It was not. The children's phrase about sticks and stones were as threatening as Miss Mondey was capable. Insults like hers only work on the petty elites and the weakminded lowest dregs.

"Fine, then. I take your point." Daniels gave a surrendering nod. "Just remind me never to piss you off. I like you better as an annoying soused wolf."

"That so?" James gave a hammed-up wink to the Inspector. Daniels didn't even skip a beat and slapped the affluent idiot across his cheek. Boggs looked like a surprised child who was standing aside as his parents fought. "Well, not the first slap I've received, not likely to be the last." James shrugged.

"Keep it up. I'm ambidextrous." Daniels lifted his other hand, making James take a single step out of reach. The Inspector folded his arms again and tilted his head.

"So what now, sirs?" asked Boggs.

"*Now*, I perform my greatest feat of acting by playing the outraged aristocrat who insists on a stay of the charges for his *dear sister*." James draped an arm over his forehead in an overly theatrical way. "Hm, if this goes well, maybe my next option is to try and get into the moving pictures to save my lifestyle."

It would be no difficult task to convince Blofeld to hold off on closing this case. He was always *so* eager to please someone of influence. The three of them trekked across the building, directing James to Blofeld's office. James cleared his throat and smoothed his hair to create an air of respectability about him. He took a few huffs and puffs before pounding on the door!

"What the-" Blofeld began before the door was flung open by James!

"Are *you* in charge here!?" James shouted as Daniels followed him, also putting on an act for Blofeld's benefit.

He feigned trying to chase after and hold back James as he approached the Chief Inspector's desk. James stormed up and slammed both hands onto it.

"What's the meaning of this, young man!?" Blofeld stood up in an outrage.

"Terribly sorry, sir. This is James Mondey." said Daniels as a look of sudden recognition spread across Blofeld's face.

"Oh, Mr Mondey. A pleasure to-" He began to outstretch his hand but it was rudely swatted away by James.

"You're charging my sister with *murder!?*" He snapped.

"Well, she was taken in with a designated murder weapon in her possession. We had no choice but to keep her for questioning." Blofeld was nervously adjusting his tie.

James continued a verbal barrage, barely letting Blofeld get a word in, until he agreed to hold off on the charges. It was exceptionally cathartic for Daniels to see someone letting loose on his superior. He always wanted to do something like this to him, but for now, Gabriel had to live vicariously through his American companion. Perhaps James was onto something with that idea of acting in films. He almost had Daniels believing that he cared about Elsbeth.

Thus, we return once again to Everjust, where the arrival of Mr and Mrs Cole sent Essie Cyrus into an eager sprint to open the front door for the pair.

"*Bonjour*, Essie!" cried Amelia with a wave. Her husband took her arm and they hastily approached Everjust to enter through the awaiting door. "So what was so important that James insisted we come immediately?"

"Yes, where is the old boy?" Spencer queried as he leaned into the lounge.

"Oh, he's not here at the moment." Essie replied. Amelia flicked her sun shades off of her face and peered from beneath her brow.

"*Eh?*" She queried. "*Tu veux dire*, that we came all this way and he just *foutu* to who knows where?" Amelia seemed exceptionally put out.

"Language, love." Spencer stroked her shoulder.

"Well, um," Essie tried to think of how to quell Mrs Cole's wrath toward James for this perceived lapse in manners. "Something urgent had come up and-"

"His sister, Miss Elsbeth, was arrested for the murder of Mr Hammond." Cecil chimed in. Both Coles seemed surprised but maintained stoic stances, even though their expressions looked like a pair of stunned fighters. "Miss Karras has only just left to rejoin Susan after the two of us found out that the mysterious Mr Spinner was the purchaser of the telltale explosive that knocked you flatter than a crêpe."

"That is stereotypical." The couple stated to Cecil in unison.

"Whatever you say. Mr Wood has also found that Mr Spinner's perceived company does not exactly exist. Mondey asked you here to take a look at this little piece." Cecil waved after them to follow him into the lounge.

"My, you lot *have* been busy." The French woman chuckled.

Mr Wood handed his butler the brick of metal that was sitting next to him on the side table. He was simply sitting in his chair, smoking a pipe, which Cecil wafted his hand toward.

"Roland, if you're going to do that, won't you please confine it to your quarters and crack the window?" He snipped.

"Technically, this whole house is my quarters, Cecil." Mr Wood chided, much to Amelia and Essie's amusement. Cecil's only reply was to move to the side of the room, grumbling complaints to himself.

Professor Cole took the brick in hand himself and examined it closely. He even pulled out his pince-nez glasses to take a magnified look at the style of the metal. Spencer began walking around with it, pondering, while Mr Wood held the bottle of paint up in his free hand.

"This was found along with it." He stated, handing the bottle to Amelia.

"*Qu'est-ce que c'est?*" She asked as she took the bottle by its lid and gave it a small shake. She then twisted the lid off and dipped the tip of her small finger into the bottle. "*Intéressant.*" Amelia rubbed the small spot of paint between her pinkie and thumb, taking note of the texture and colour.

"What is it, Amelia?" Essie peered, close by her side.

"It is paint for metal, but it's cheap. Disgustingly cheap." Amelia sneered. "Not to say that choosing something affordable is, eh, *mauvais*—um, bad, but this is the lowest possible quality that someone might use to mask tarnishing to make it look newer than it is."

"So, shoddy shyster's paint?" Mr Wood queried for specifications.

"Something that would make *you* walk away in second-hand embarrassment." Amelia chuckled as she pointed at Mr Wood.

"Shoddy paint and a chunk of cheap, soft metal." Spencer finally spoke up. "I'll try to restrain my long-winded and advanced phraseology that often causes my testimonies to be lost-"

"You are failing, *mon amour.*" Amelia snapped her fingers and shook her head with an amused smile as her husband attempted to get his proverbial train of thought back onto its rails.

"Yes, um. This metal, bottom line, is cheap and soft." He stated. "Where was this found?"

"Hidden under Tilmann's forge and wrapped inside his apron." Mr Wood explained.

"Ah, then that is why James asked me about that fellow. I had suspicions about him." Spencer flicked his hand. "Not of *murder* mind you, but if that fellow thought he was going to fool any of us with *this*," Spencer laughed, truly amused like he was reading a comical novel.

"*Encore moins avec ça!*" Amelia held up the bottle with a smirk, inferring that the paint would have been an equal giveaway.

"I think I'm understanding his thought process, though." Mr Wood nodded. "Bear with me. Tilmann uses the soft metal and makes it more malleable in the heat of the forge, his intention to *mold* and *shape* his creation rather than actually *forge* it."

"Because he hasn't a clue how," Essie interjected. Mr Wood snapped his fingers and pointed to her, indicating that she was absolutely correct!

"Then, after shaping his effigy hilt, he masks his fraudulent move by painting it to look like a different metal." Mr Wood continued.

"This would never have dried in time." It was Amelia's turn to weigh in an opinion this time. "Upon examination, he'd have been disqualified the moment the paint came off on any of the judges' hands."

"Well, would that have dried if he held it near to the heat?" Mr Wood smiled knowingly. Amelia's silence spoke volumes.

"But there's one problem, Mr Wood." Spencer chimed back in. "We were watching him as much as any other contestant. Myself even more so because of his shifty actions. We would have noticed all this skullduggery."

"True. You *would* have unless something would have happened to draw your attention." Mr Wood took another small puff of his pipe. "Something like a forge bursting into flame?"

The whole room went silent. Cecil was the only one who was ready to speak up as he didn't seem to follow such a thought. It didn't add up. Cecil stepped forward, swaying his watch curiously.

"But how would he have known that such a thing would happen if it was Mr Spinner who caused the explosion?" asked Cecil with an air that reminded Spencer of an arrogant student of his, always correcting his classmates.

"I'm still working on the finer details, but as far as we know, Mr Spinner was hinting at an '*accident*' that was likely to happen, to anyone who would listen." Mr Wood finally sat his pipe aside on its mount, which Cecil immediately sprinted over and grabbed to have it cleaned out. He chuckled. "There are just far too many loose ends that only make sense if you tie them together."

"True," said Spencer, removing his glasses. "Apart, these things make a series of strange coincidences. I believe we all know what a series of coincidences is."

"More mythical than the things in your last exposition." Essie completed the thought, to which every member in the room nodded along.

"And while I may have no more love lost for James's family than he does, I don't intend to let a killer get off scot-free." Mr Wood gently bounced his fist on the arm of his chair.

"Knowing James, he's undoubtedly of the same mind." Amelia smirked as she watched Cecil frantically try to scrape out the pipe.

"Darling? I think I'd like to speak with this fellow, Tilmann." Spencer weighed the chunk of metal in his hand.

"Well, why don't we all go? We can take my car." Mr Wood finally removed himself from his seat as he gestured to Essie.

"I'm permitted to come this time?" She bounded on her heels.

"Of course. The only reason I had Cecil keep you here was so that you wouldn't charge off like a would-be knight in shining armour and endanger yourself." Mr Wood explained as he slipped past everyone to get to the foyer. "You're coming too, Cecil!"

"Oh, *goodie!*" The butler snapped sarcastically. He charged into the foyer, still cleaning the pipe until Essie snatched it from his hands and tossed it back into the lounge. Cecil stared hard into the room with a twitch in his eye. "If any ash gets on that furniture, you're reup-holstering it." Essie's only reply was to toss his coat over his head which he immediately pulled off and donned it normally. "Are you *ever* going to stop giving me the cold shoulder?"

Essie's only reply was a coy smirk over her shoul-der as she stepped outside to await Mr Wood, who had gone after the Horch himself. Cecil cricked his neck, an idiosyncrasy he'd never had before, as he turned to call into the kitchen.

"Cook! We're heading out! Keep dinner warm and we'll return shortly!" He cried out only to be met with clanging pots as a reply. "Very good." Cecil adjusted his coat and left to wait in an awkward silence alongside Essie, much to Amelia's amusement.

Chapter Ten

The Coles returned to their car while Mr Wood took the wheel of the Horch, checking the fuel gauge, as the car had been used quite a bit recently. There was just enough for the errands he was going on today. Mr Wood led the way to the inn considering he was the only one of the lot who knew the exact address. He was the one who set the contestants up in their rooms under James's name, and he had a sneaking suspicion that yet another room was soon to be vacated. Upon arriving at the inn, the Criminology Society exited their respective vehicles and Professor Cole led the way into the building.

"Essie, Cec, I want the two of you to keep an eye on the outside." Mr Wood directed his employees. "There's a door around back, I want *you* there Cecil."

"Um, might it be prudent for us to remain together?" Cecil attempted to persuade Mr Wood to consider a different approach, but not for the reasons you might think.

"Solve your little spat in your off hours, please. We need to have as much coverage as possible." Cecil's face turned red as a cherry at Mr Wood's comment, which made Essie have to stifle her laughter.

The indignant butler stormed around back via the garden while the remaining Society members entered the inn. Professor Cole led the pack walking up to the front desk and ringing the bell.

"I'm coming!" The sharp voice of the old woman who owned the place came piercing through the door behind the desk. She hobbled out of the room and took her place on the stool. "What can I help you with?"

"I'm here to see Mr Tilmann, I-"

"Oh! I've had just about enough of this inquisition! All these people traipsing about my home without a care, to say nothing of not shelling out a shilling for marking up the floors!" The woman was on a nonstop rant which caused Spencer to shrink back to the group and slip behind his wife. "And on top of all that, what have I to show for all this nonsense? A dead body in my lovely garden!" Amelia was about to light into this old crone, if not for making Spencer nervous then to just have her shut up! Mr Wood patted her shoulder though.

"Flora, Flora." Mr Wood spoke with a gentle tone and his signature kindly smile. The old woman adjusted her glasses as she looked upward at the massive figure.

"Oh, Mr Wood!" Her demeanour had turned to a complete flip of what everyone had seen so far. Suddenly she was the sweetest little granny anyone could meet. "So lovely to see you, dearie!"

"You as well, my fine lady. I do apologize for the circumstances that you've had to endure." He replied.

"I should hope so." The old woman crossed her arms.

"Indeed, and I'll be glad to compensate you further for the inconvenience this has caused you." He went on further. "And whilst we discuss that, my associate would like a word with Mr Tilmann. Which room might he be in?"

The lady adjusted her glasses to look over her hen scratch and Mr Wood leaned over, impairing her view of the others. He discretely waved his hand behind his back, signalling Spencer to go. It was going to be easier to knock on the doors than charm information out of this senile and ill-tempered lady.

Amelia gently grabbed her husband's arm and they quietly slunk to the side while the embittered woman had her nose in her registry. The couple crossed the dining room and ascended the stairs, being careful to avoid any creaking steps while Mr Wood kept the woman busy. While Spencer and Amelia crossed the upstairs hallway, one of the doors opened.

"Oh!" Miss Ware started to close her door but Mrs Cole gently placed her hand on it. She might know which room was Tilmann's, and if not, she might still have something useful to mention without knowing.

"*Mademoiselle* Ware?" Amelia put slight pressure on the door; only enough to keep her from closing it.

"W-who are you?"

"She's my wife, Miss Ware." Spencer tugged at Amelia's sleeve to point out that she was frightening the poor girl.

"Oh, Mr Cole. I'm glad to see you're feeling better." She smiled weakly. "I'm sorry, do come in." She finally opened the door. "I'm sorry. These happenings have me so frazzled." She took a drink of water from a glass. Amelia noticed a bottle of medicine next to it.

"You are trying to calm yourself, I see." She pointed to the bottle of light sedatives. "I give my husband those when he works too late," Amelia smirked.

"Excuse me?" Spencer cocked his brow. Amelia simply ruffled his messy light hair in reply.

"Yes, Mr McClain was kind enough to bring them to me. Well, I'm sure you can understand my worries if they've told you about it." The timid young lady sighed. Amelia looked at the woman with a caring expression as she reminded her a great deal of her dear friend Susan.

"We *have* been appraised of the situation, yes." Spencer bent down to pat her hand. "I'm so sorry you have to go through this ordeal."

"It feels foolish to be so unstrung by this considering *you* were in the thick of it at the park." Sara chuckled nervously, trying to assuage her anxiety.

"Believe me, dear, that's far and away not the worst thing we've seen." Spencer rubbed his hand over where he had been bandaged. "So, if I may ask, what made you poke your head into the hall? Were you expecting somebody?" Sara went silent as the grave as she did in fact look like she had something to say.

"*Fini, ma chérie.*" Amelia bid her.

"Well..." She paused. "I was rather hoping it would be Mr Mondey or the Inspector. But the two of you have a connection to them as well, yes?" Her voice sounded eager, but she was beginning to look completely worn out. It could have been either the emotions or the tranquillizers that she had just taken. Possibly a combination of the two.

"Go on." Spencer gave Sara's shoulder a nudge.

"It was something that I... I heard while... everybody was giving their state... ments." Her face began to look a bit flushed. Sara placed a hand on her head as the room seemed to spin. "Something didn't make sense... I-" It was at this point that the poor girl collapsed! Professor Cole managed to catch her, but not being as physically inclined as James or Mr Wood, he stumbled back with the girl in hand!

"Miss Ware!?" Spencer was no medical man, but he knew enough to tell that the girl's breathing was dangerously laboured.

Amelia jumped to aid Spencer in laying the girl down gently. She turned and looked at the bottle of nerve medicine, pouring a few of the pills into her hand.

"*C'est faux!* The pills do not match the label!" Amelia exclaimed.

"Help! Someone, help!" Spencer screamed to the closed door, still trying to hold Miss Ware's head upright.

The door opened and there stood Tilmann and Jaqueline, who had both come running from their rooms when they heard the commotion.

"Miss Brush! Help us get her up." Spencer begged the larger woman, who sprung immediately to action.

"Tilmann, call for an ambulance!" Mrs Cole barked at him. "It will go a long way to mend our opinions of your character."

"What's that supposed to mean?" Tilmann questioned, looking distraught with all that was going on all of a sudden.

"*Allez-y maintenant!*" Mrs Cole bellowed louder, making the well-dressed charlatan back into the wall before rounding out of the doorway to find the nearest phone.

Heavy footsteps, likely those of Mr Wood, could be heard downstairs.

"Mr and Mrs Cole!?" cried Mr Wood's voice. "What on earth is happening!?"

"It's Miss Ware! We think she's been poisoned!" Spencer cried back while attempting to help Jaqueline lift the young woman up.

"This is gettin' to be one hell of an ordeal." Miss Brush groaned as she carried Sara out of her room and down the hall. Tilmann returned from completing Mrs Cole's order.

"They're on their way!" He ran his fingers through his hair, stressed as could be. "We didn't lose *another* one, did we?" His breathing was heavy and he clutched at the back of his head.

"She's still breathing at the moment, I think." Professor Cole stood hand to mouth. "I'm really not *that kind* of expert."

"*Ne t'inquiète pas*, *mon amour*, our friends will help that poor girl." Amelia stroked her husband's cheek waiting for Jaqueline to successfully descend the stairs to meet Mr Wood and wait for the ambulance.

Amelia waited for the group to be out of sight before she directed her more negatively passionate demeanour toward the weasely little man standing with them. "Now, *ami*, let's have a small chat with you, *allons-nous?*" She pressed Tilmann's shoulder against the wall.

"Darling! I don't think now is really the time!" Spencer tried to draw his wife away, but she was still locked onto her quarry.

"I don't trust any other time, I trust here and now." She stared hard at the man as she held his vest tightly.

"Get off me, you frog!" Tilmann tried to swat Amelia's hand away, but that only resulted in her drawing him back and pushing him into the wall yet again, this time with a bump to the head.

"Call me that again and you will not like how this ends." She smirked.

"What next? You're going to bludgeon me with a bottle of wine?" Tilmann griped at her as he rubbed his head.

"*Non, tu as mal comprise*. I am not the one whose wrath you will incur." She nodded her head at the androgynous little man behind her, who was staring a hole through Tilmann's head.

Tilmann was taken aback to see such a searing expression on the nervous little man who spoke at the convention. Spencer was less than pleased about this slimy little con artist having the audacity to insult his wife in such a way. He stepped closer to his wife's side and pointed his index finger at the tip of Tilmann's nose.

"We have irrefutable proof that you made an attempt to cheat in the competition." Spencer's voice was steady and unfaltering with a hostile low hiss in his voice. He couldn't bellow like his wife or Mr Wood, but apparently, he didn't *need* to.

"I don't think that's the most-" He was pressed against the wall once more.

"What's more, we suspect that your entry into the competition was falsified." The Professor hissed once again. "Given all that's come to light, it stands to reason that from this point on, you are forthwith disqualified from the competition!" Tilmann's eyes widened.

"Wait! Don't be too hasty in that type of decision, now!" Tilmann chuckled nervously. "Please, I need that prize. I can't go on working in a watch shop forever, I want to work for the Woodland Company!" He kept going on pleading his case but the Coles looked at one another before cutting the little man off.

"Hang on," Spencer jumped in, placing his hand on Tilmann's chest. "What makes you think that you would work for Mr Wood?"

Tilmann froze up for just a moment, not knowing how to talk his way out of this one. His eyes darted between the cultured couple, trying to think of any excuse he could. Instead, he was saved by the call of Mr Wood.

"Get back down here, you two!" He cried from the base of the stairs.

Amelia narrowed her eyes at Tilmann and begrudgingly released him. He straightened his vest as the pair descended the stairs.

When the Coles came downstairs they could see that Jaqueline was carrying Sara outside followed by Mr Wood. He waved them over as they were heading out to wait for the ambulance and give Miss Ware some fresh air. Essie was in a tizzy, worried about the young metalworker.

"Did either of you manage to find Tilmann?" asked Mr Wood.

"We had... *words* with him, *oui*." Amelia spoke with her arms crossed.

"Hmm," Mr Wood's face sank a bit. "Follow-up question, then; Is he the next body?" Spencer shook his head in the negative.

"No, but he is most definitely out of the competition for his actions. What concerns me is that he somehow knew about the prize being a position in the Woodland Company." He explained, keeping his voice low, prompting a rise in the jolly gentleman's eyebrows.

Mr Wood's eyes drifted to the second floor of the building. Tilmann's room was not in the front, but it was easy to know why he would look up there with that pondering look on his face. His thoughts might have kept going, but the sound of shrill sirens grew loud enough that he couldn't ignore it. The ambulance was arriving to pick up Sara.

As the medics helped to load the poor girl into the vehicle, Essie noticed something in the corner of her eye. She attempted to be discreet in peering to her side, also noticing that Spencer was doing the same. They both looked at each other and the Professor gave a subtle nod. They both could see that Kent McClain was hiding in the bushes in the garden, not far from where Hammond was found.

"Why is he hiding?" Essie queried in a whisper.

"According to Miss Ware, Mr McClain was the one who brought her the nerve pills that caused this reaction." Spencer's eyes had lingered on Kent for a moment too long, as Kent left the bushes, trying to keep low.

Essie noticed and immediately moved to follow! Spencer clicked his tongue and followed her. The two of them crossed the side of the inn but Professor Cole held Essie back as they reached the rear corner. They could hear two voices.

"Mr McClain." Came the dulcet tones of Cecil. "Alright?"

"Yeah, mate, just uh, taking a stroll through the garden," McClain replied, his voice shaky and nervous. "So, what's your mates doing here, eh?"

"Looking to have a word with Mr Tilmann. They've found some evidence that he was cheating in the competition." Cecil explained to the scarred man. "Low on priorities, I realize, but I believe they hope he will incriminate himself in an attempt of sabotage."

"Oh, aye?" McClain's voice was still uneven, but there was something else suspicious in his tone. The mention of Tilmann brought up a slightly hostile brogue.

Essie broke free of Spencer's grip and rounded the corner.

"On that note, why is Sara being taken to hospital because of the pills you gave her?" McClain was taken off guard by the sudden appearance of the brash maid.

"Beg pardon?" Cecil raised his brow, his eyes shifting to Kent. "Mr McClain-" Before Cec could finish the thought, the smith decked him and made a run for the fence behind the house!

Spencer immediately ran over to Cecil, who was knocked clean off his feet, but Essie gave chase! Kent kicked off the ground and jumped onto the fence, using his momentum to fling himself over the top. Essie lifted the hem of her dress and made an attempt to follow, which might have worked except her height, or lack thereof, became a hindrance. Essie managed to grab the top of the fence but bounced off the wooden barrier like a tennis ball while dressing her palms with splinters.

"*Hellfire!*" Essie cried out as she curled on the ground while clutching her hands.

Cecil perked up quickly and pushed Spencer aside to run to Essie's aid. He knelt down and gently pulled her hands apart, taking a look at her scuffed and punctured palms.

"Miss Cyrus, you pint-sized twit! Why would you *do* that!?" Cecil pulled a handkerchief from his pocket and wrapped one of her hands. Essie mumbled as Cecil reached invasively into the Professor's pocket and appropriated *his* handkerchief to wrap her other hand. "This kind of reckless behaviour is exactly why Mr Wood had me keep you at the house, so you wouldn't go around harming yourself to chase after suspects in *murder investigations!* What do you have to say for yourself?" Essie just looked at him, masking her negativity with a charming smile.

"I only do this when I have *you* nearby." She gave him a strange but kind '*look*' with her eyes which made his face go red. Cecil tried to think up a reply, but he sputtered like a malfunctioning engine.

"So which one of you will explain this to Mr Wood?" Spencer chimed in, turning both of their faces pale.

"Explain what?"

Mr Wood came running over, taking a look at the scene before him. He crossed his arms across his barrel chest and looked down at the three.

"I simply cannot take my eyes off of you for half a moment, can I?" Mr Wood looked at the fence and down at Essie. Cecil remained frozen in place as though he was hoping he would remain unseen by keeping still. "So, what happened?"

"Kent McClain made a grand escape." Professor Cole began but was cut off by Mr Wood's immediate understanding.

"I see, the rest is evident." Mr Wood placed his hand on the stiff butler's head. "You didn't try to stop her?"

"I chased Mr McClain after he struck Cecil. I hardly gave him a chance to stop me." Essie could see that Mr Wood was only having a bit of fun at Cecil's expense, but he was also taking the current events very seriously.

"So McClain is on the run?" Mr Wood stroked his beard.

"It seems we may have to rethink the theory on what happened." Spencer assessed the issue. Mr Wood gave a single stroke to his beard, along with a confirming nod.

"Hmm, either way, we should contact Inspector Daniels. Hopefully, this will also draw some suspicion away from Elsbeth Mondey." Mr Wood lifted Cecil back to his feet, who in turn, helped up Essie. "Come along, all." Mr Wood led the way back to the ambulance.

"Where in blazes were you lot?" Amelia queried to the group as they all began to gather by the cars.

"A rather long story for such quick events." Spencer sighed as he took his wife's hands. She spotted Essie's injuries and flew into a protective panic.

"*Mon dieu*, Essie, *qui t'a fait ça!?*" Amelia bellowed, swapping out her husband's hands for her friend's. "*Je veux leur sang!*"

"I'll explain later." Spencer rubbed her shoulders, hoping to quell her wrath as she was out for revenge against whoever harmed Essie. First her husband, now her young friend? *Someone* was going to pay dearly.

"This case continues to unravel like a wool sweater with a loose thread." Cecil huffed in an ever-growing frustration.

"On the contrary, Cecil," Mr Wood patted his butler's shoulder. "It may seem as though things are falling apart, but I haven't given up on my standing theory yet." Cecil moved Mr Wood's hand off of his shoulder and straightened his jacket.

"Forgive me, Roland, but it seems to me that all of our theories keep flipping more than James's mattress." Mr Wood stifled a laugh but turned to face Cecil.

"An upturn in events does not change the thought process that I intend to follow." He looked to the inn itself. "I'll have to stay here to smooth things over with Flora, and I also want to keep an eye on Tilmann; assure him that the Coles were a bit hasty and hope he'll stay where I can keep an eye on him."

"And the rest of us?" Cecil was concerned with the fact that he was only including himself in this.

"If you're concerned about my safety, I intend to call up Daniels and let him know of the situation. In addition, I'd like for you to take care of Essie's hands at home while the Coles have a word with some of their transit contacts. If McClain is on the run for fear of harming Sara

Ware, he's likely to try and escape Oxford altogether." Mr Wood walked past everyone as he returned to the inn.

Cecil turned his attention to the Coles.

"'Transit connections'?" He asked.

"We often must have friends in the right places to ensure that either investors or items of importance arrive, eh, safe and concise." Amelia illustrated her point with a rub of her fingers.

"We should head to the station straight away, my love." Spencer tugged at her hand. Mrs Cole nodded in agreement and they rushed to their car.

"And what is it we're meant to do?" Essie asked.

"Mr Wood requested that we go back home to doctor up those hands of yours." Cecil turned her by her shoulders toward the Horch. "Get in."

Following these events, we find James Mondey in the office of Inspector Daniels at the station. The two were chuckling to themselves as Daniels poured over the notes he and Boggs had taken on the case so far.

"I have to say, James, you nearly had *me* convinced that you actually wanted your sister out of our custody." Daniels smiled, still staring at the papers. "I haven't seen Blofeld tug at his collar that much since his wife came for a visit."

"*Ha!*" James leaned back in his chair letting out his signature laugh. "Maybe I was onto something with that motion picture idea, eh?"

"Maybe so." Daniels shrugged. His phone began to ring which he immediately answered. "Inspector Daniels speaking." James could hear a deep voice on the other end of the call. Whoever it was just gave the Inspector some grave news because he shot up from his chair like a broken bedspring! "What!? When!?"

"Hm?" James was met with an index finger held in his face.

"I'll be over shortly! Don't you move!" Daniels put the receiver back on the hook and he dropped his head while leaning on his desk. "This job is going to age me a decade before this case is over."

"What's going on, old man?"

"Somebody just attempted to poison Sara Ware. That was your friend, Wood. He's at the inn as we speak." It was James's turn to pop out of his seat, but instead of hopping straight up, he launched himself at the office door.

"What are we waiting for, then!? We should already be halfway to the car!" James poked his head out of the office. "Boggs! Grab your helmet!"

Daniels cleared his throat to ensure that James knew who was truly in charge here. The boys collected their constable and ran to the back-and-white garage. Daniels took the wheel to ensure they reached the inn quickly, siren blaring the entire way.

"I am telling you right now, it wasn't Kent McClain." James insisted as he rode with folded arms in the speeding vehicle. He was rather relaxed while Boggs was holding onto his safety belt.

"I only offered you the information that Mr Wood gave *me*, Mondey." Daniels sighed as the entire drive so far had been filled with James's objections.

"Yeah, I know, but there's no way he could be behind harming Sara Ware." James coiled himself so tight in his seat that he looked like a threatened snake.

"If you'll excuse me but how can you tell, Mr Mondey?" Boggs chimed in.

"First of all, I was under the impression you couldn't even speak, I haven't heard you say a word anytime that I've been near you. Kudos on surprising me." James gave a crooked smile as he turned his head to the constable while still maintaining his solid pouting stance. "Secondly, it's his hands."

"His... hands?" Boggs was curious about what James meant about that. Daniels was as well, but with a guarded expectation that this was likely to go somewhere infuriating.

"Didn't you notice the way he handles things in them?"

"No, James," Daniels spoke through gritted teeth. "Nobody but you would have noticed that, and if this goes to yet another one of your opportunistic euphemisms I swear to the Lord in heaven, I'm kicking you *out* of this moving vehicle."

"It's not a euphemism, it's simple social deduction— His hands, though scarred by fire, are gentle and dextrous. That man has never raised his hands in a violent manner in his life. Believe me, if anyone knows how to judge someone by their hands, *it's me.* And for your information, *that* was a euphemism." James smirked only to be met with a glare and a growl.

"Need I remind you that the possible method of harm was poison?" Daniels pointed out after calming himself with a sigh.

"Yes, the favoured weapon of those who are either clever or cowardly, and while this may sound derogatory, Kent McClain is neither." James held up two fingers. "His scars and the way he presents them so freely is proof he is no coward." He lowered one finger. "And while I mean no offence by stating this, he is not intelligent to the correct degree. He's a practical artist, he makes creative metal objects for whatever someone wants. He's clever, but not remotely to a malicious degree."

"People don't always kill based on logic or reason, James." Daniels glanced at James in the mirror once again. The clever carouser once again raised two fingers. "Oh, here we go again."

"If that was the case, he would either need a proper motive or he would be a perfect example of psychopathy." James smiled once more. "I'd go further, but we seem to have arrived." He pointed out the window at the upcoming inn.

No sooner had they parked when Mr Wood opened the front door and waved at them. The three fellows quickly met him at the inn's opening.

"Well, the plot continues to thicken." Mr Wood nodded.

"Any plot that puts me in contact with you people seems to turn into a maze of solid walls." Daniels breathed a sigh of exasperation. "Now where is Mr McClain?"

"On the run, I'm afraid. When Miss Ware was taken in the ambulance he fled for self-preservation."

"Then why did you ask us here!? Give me that phone!" Daniels ran in and grabbed the telephone from the front desk. He began demanding a line to the station so that he could have a bulletin put out on Kent McClain.

"I confess, I'm a little stumped why you had us come if that was the case." James added with Boggs by his side.

"The reasoning has a few layers." Mr Wood began. "I'm less concerned with McClain getting away since the Coles are calling in their transit contacts—by now they'll have any train lines or shipping services watching for him. Another is that I wanted to compare notes on what we have so far. Finally, I wanted to confer *here* because Tilmann is in his room and I think it will go a ways to keep him scared stiff with police in the house." He shifted his eyes toward Boggs which was also referential to Inspector Daniels.

"Ah, I see." James tapped the side of his nose with a knowing grin. "Well, for starters, we kept them from proceeding with pinning this on my sister. Oh! And I have a brand new reason to hate her more than the devil himself." James said so with a chipper smile, but the burning rage was easy to see behind it.

"A feat, indeed." Mr Wood lowered his brows, thinking of how that could even be plausible.

"Yes, my sister was found with the bloodied hammer that killed Hammond because she wanted to plant it somewhere to incriminate me, *just* to cause problems." Mr Wood was speechless at that. Something like that was on a level of immoral that he didn't think a Mondey capable of! "I know. Stupid on an unimaginable scale."

"Well, come along." Mr Wood led James and Boggs in past the Inspector to have a seat in the dining room. "I'll tell you about things on our end." Boggs pulled out his notebook to log every ounce of information for the case and for Inspector Daniels to review later.

Around the same time that Mr Wood began catching the boys up on the events they missed, Cecil and Essie arrived home at Everjust. Their ride was completely silent, but not from any hard feelings—just general awkwardness. Cecil had become too afraid that he would say something else to dig his hole further and Essie was thoroughly entertained by it. His suffering was beginning to lose its charm, though, and she thought that once they got inside she would end his suffering, mostly because Essie was starting to feel the pain in her hands at last as the adrenaline had run out. They parked the Horch and slipped into the house through the kitchen.

"Go pop into the lounge, I'll bring in some fix-its for your hands." Cecil guided her along.

"Okay." Essie smiled with a small wince from the stinging in her palms and fingers.

Cecil knew better than to clean wounds in the kitchen as Cook would have his hide. The only thing he wondered was where she was while he retrieved an injury kit from the pantry. It was still hours before Cook would go home, so her whereabouts were something of a mystery.

"*Cecil!*" Essie screamed from the other room! Mr Blackbird whipped around and bolted through the foyer. He hurried to Essie, who was standing in the lounge archway. Upon running to her side he looked in the lounge and saw a man sitting in Mr Wood's chair.

"Good afternoon." The man's face and voice were familiar. It was the man that they'd spoken to at the park. Before them sat the elusive Mr Spinner!

Chapter Eleven

Cecil immediately pushed Essie behind him, putting himself between the dear maid and Mr Spinner. The man smiled in response to the defensive move and remained seated. He had his legs crossed as he eyed the two from Mr Wood's favourite chair. He was wearing a very nice double-breasted pinstripe suit with his hat sitting on the arm of his chosen seat. His thin moustache lined his crooked smile which was very unfamiliar from the man they were speaking to the day of the '*accident*'. All things considered, though, he was unmistakably the same man.

"I see you still haven't learned to properly adjust a tie." Cecil sneered, pointing out that his neckwear was still quite crooked. "Now as the home retainer, I must inform you that you are unwelcome and if you do not leave I shall have to call the proper authorities." He spoke sternly with his gaze unblinking and hard. Spinner smiled once again, turning his nose up.

"Mr Wood has a very nice home, here." Spinner's gaze turned up to the high ceiling. He looked as though he was admiring the architecture. Neither Cecil nor Essie were confused by his veiled compliment, as a statement like that is only ever meant as a threat.

"Indeed, and I should hate to have to clean blood out of the rug." Essie spoke up, equally as cold.

"Then I'll be brief." Mr Spinner stood up, brushing his index finger along his pencil moustache. His expression remained calm but brusque as he flashed a snide grin. "Stop your intrusions into the case. Let things run their due course and forget about me. *I'm* not the one who blew up that forge." Essie stepped forward but Cecil held his hand in front of her to keep her from stepping up to a dangerous figure again.

"But you planted the idea, didn't you?" She asked with an accusatory tone. Mr Spinner turned his head aside and grinned.

"I'm sure I haven't a clue what you mean, dear. And a court of law mightn't either." He glanced toward the pair.

"If you're so innocent, I'm sure you wouldn't mind waiting here for the police to have a word." Cecil was preparing to close the hidden sliding doors in the archway to seal him in but before the persnickety butler could shut the doors, Mr Spinner pointed a single-shot pistol at Miss Cyrus!

"I'm afraid I'll be otherwise engaged, my good man." Spinner cocked his brow like some dashing rogue in a moving picture. He motioned his armed hand over indicating the pair to step aside. They had no choice but to oblige as neither wanted the other to be harmed.

Spinner sauntered past them into the foyer after putting on his hat, keeping his eye on them. His snide grin was fascinating to Essie because when they spoke to him at the park, he gave *no* indications that he was a suspicious figure whatsoever. His acting skills were so well cultivated that he could be making a fortune in a gambler's den, yet instead, he was here making threats to a couple of curious domestics.

He was watching them both very closely, keeping that smug expression as he opened the door. Behind him, however, were Susan and Andrea! The latter of the ladies assessed the situation quickly and kicked the back of Spinner's leg, causing him to drop down to one knee with a pained shout. Susan, also thinking fast despite her shock at the situation, made use of the closed parasol clutched in her hand and used the crook of the handle to snag his arm!

Cecil ran to the doorway to apprehend the man after he dropped his pistol and tackled him, causing both men to roll down the stoop! Cecil struck the man across the jaw with his fist but Spinner replied with a knee between the butler's legs.

"*Agh!*" Cecil rolled off of Spinner, clutching his injured *in-betweens*. This allowed the villainous figure to scramble to his feet in an attempt to make a run for it!

Essie jumped from the stoop with Spinner's gun in her injured hand and attempted to hold the weapon steady despite the pain in her palm. She squeezed the trigger and a sharp pop sounded on Holywell Street. Spinner's shoulder reacted! He nearly fell forward but kept on running. There was no way that the Society members were going to catch up with him, especially when their first concern was Cecil and Essie with their clear injuries. Susan and Andrea got on either side of Cecil and helped him up.

"Are you alright, Mr Blackbird?" Susan asked with a worried pitch.

"I just took a knee clad in blended fabric to the most sensitive area on my entire body." Cecil's voice was strained as he choked out his sardonic statement. "Does that sound '*alright*'?"

"Don't be unkind, Cec, she's showing concern!" Essie snapped at him, wincing as she let the pistol hang loosely on her finger.

"Did that bloke do that!?" Andrea growled.

"No, this happened from chasing another suspect." Essie presented her wrapped hands.

"Alright, come along, we'll patch this up. Susan dear, can you help Cec inside?" Andrea asked as she watched the poor man try to lumber back to the house, hunched over. Susan aided him to the best of her ability by bracing his arm while Andrea led Essie inside by her fingertips.

Once back inside the safety of the house, Cecil sprawled out on the couch in the lounge with Susan fussing over him.

"The medical supplies are in the kitchen awaiting retrieval, Andie." Cecil instructed her with a stiff groan framing his voice.

"Excellent, c'mon luv." Andrea and Essie made their way to the kitchen.

Miss Karras managed to find all the pieces she would need after taking a look at what was under the handkerchiefs around Essie's hands. Susan had joined the ladies after Cecil insisted that he would be fine on his own to recover.

"My, that looks painful." Susan fanned herself.

"It certainly wasn't comfortable." Essie mused with a chuckle.

"This is going to need some iodine. It's going to hurt like all hell, but it'll do you better than putting up with an infection. Won't be cleaning much if you have no hands." Andrea looked around.

"It won't be here, the iodine is in the washroom upstairs." Essie pointed at the ceiling, illustrating the upstairs.

"I've got it." Susan left the kitchen to find the bottle while Andrea prepared some tweezers to begin pulling out the splinters of wood.

"What the hell is all this?" She questioned the amount of wooden shrapnel in the young woman's palms. "You look as though you were fighting off a tree."

"I tried to make a leap for the fence behind the inn. It didn't work, since I'm not much of an Olympic athlete." Essie replied.

"Right, but why the hell did you *do* it?" Andrea laughed at the absurdity.

"Kent McClain has been implicated in something. He ran and I tried to stop him. The Coles are calling in some favours to find him though." Essie winced as Andrea began picking the pieces out. She sucked air through her clenched teeth.

"I know, sorry." Andrea apologized for the obligatory stinging. "So what did he do '*allegedly*'?"

"Well, from what we know, he gave some relaxing pills to Sara Ware but we think it may have been some kind of poison." As Essie explained Andrea grew more confused but she had to remain still so she could continue carefully picking out the splinters.

"Did you see her condition?" Andrea asked.

"I saw her getting loaded into the ambulance, but not much else. The Coles were the ones who witnessed it happen."

"Come on, Essie, you're an observant girl. Think. What'd you see?" Andrea's urging took Essie's mind off of the pain in her hands as she let her mind journey back to the inn.

Essie thought hard and closed her eyes. She pictured the time when Jaqueline came through the front door with Mr Wood in tow and Sara in her arms. She looked asleep, but nothing more. Jaqueline said she was poisoned, but not by any effect had seen or read about in any of the multitudes of books in Everjust's lounge. Maybe not actual poisoning?

"She didn't look ill. She wasn't pale, no foaming at the mouth, no-" Essie's thoughts were shattered by a burning sensation! "*Ouch!*" Her eyes opened wide, noticing a damp cloth in Andrea's hand.

Next to both of them was Susan, holding a bottle. Clearly, the sought-after iodine given that Essie's hand felt like it was sitting in the fireplace.

"Sorry, again." Andrea chuckled. "So she didn't *look* poisoned? Maybe not poison, then."

"Come again?"

"In some dance halls and clubs of the like, certain types of men will slip a strong and in some cases harmful sedative into a lady's drink to make them easier to take advantage of. Commonly a high dose of Chloral Hydrate, which is the same as nerve pills but in higher doses it can be far more dangerous." She explained, horrifying the other two ladies. "On numerous occasions, it's been tried on me. Once, James caught some bloke at it and took him out back to beat him senseless."

"So she may still be in mortal danger?" Essie fussed.

"Depends on how much of the stuff she had." Andrea began unfurling some proper bandages to wrap Essie's hands in after finishing the disinfection. "Nothing to do but wait until they know for sure."

"I *hate* waiting," mumbled Essie. Susan walked over to her and rubbed her shoulder.

"I know, dear, but they do say that good things come to those who wait." She smiled to alleviate some of Essie's worry.

"But they also say that evil succeeds when the good do nothing." The petite maid offered up her counterpoint. Susan had no argument for that one. "Two, now possibly three, people are dead and we keep collecting more questions along with very few answers." The covert couple looked at each other.

"She has a point there." Said Andrea with a shrug.

"We may have a few more answers than you think." Cecil came into the kitchen, still moving a bit stiffly. "I just received a call from Mr Wood at the inn; you were all a bit preoccupied and evidently didn't hear the ringing."

That was certainly true. They all looked between themselves, silently agreeing that they hadn't heard the telephone at all. Andrea turned back to the agonized attendant.

"Well don't keep us in suspense, Cec, what did he have to say?" She goaded him to continue.

"Roland's called in James and Gabriel to swap notes. They're holding down the fort at the inn with the intent of keeping an eye on Tilmann. The boss still doesn't trust him, so they're conferring in place to have him and Jaqueline within reach." Cecil leaned his back against the doorway, likely attempting to alleviate some of the pain in his lower extremity.

"Did you tell Mr Wood about what just happened?" Essie inquired.

"Against every considerable ounce of my better judgment, I opted to omit the details for the time being." Cecil beat the back of his head lightly against the frame with every syllable. "I'm not willing to let Tilmann go without a thorough screening process either, but if we mentioned Spinner and his threats, they would be over here faster than Mercury! Best they keep a short leash on him for the time being."

"That begs the question of how we intend to find Spinner again." Andrea sighed. She rested her chin in her hand, trying to think. Susan suddenly began waving her hands excitedly.

"Oh! Darling! We saw his face, yes?" She bounded on her feet.

"That's true, but I don't-" The proverbial lightbulb switched on above Andrea's head. "You are a damned genius!"

"Can I ask for a bit of clarification?" Cecil's voice echoed Essie's thoughts, as they were both lost.

"Spencer and Amelia aren't the only ones who can call in a few favours!" Andrea had sprung from the table and rushed to grab the phone for herself. "They're watching for McClain, but *my* network of people who are sweet on me is so large, we'll have Spinner's *shoe size* in under an hour!"

The pair of domestics glanced at Miss Jordain who nodded in agreement.

"She's right." Susan put her hand on her cheek in amused admiration. Her expression changed to a thoughtful one as her hand shifted to her mouth. "I can't help but wonder how Amelia and Spencer are faring."

While the four continued to rest after yet another traumatic event to add to their growing collection, Spencer and Amelia Cole were themselves mirroring Susan's thoughts. They had put the word out to anyone they could think of and, after doing so, decided to pop into the hospital to check on Sara's condition. If they were lucky, she might be able to finish what she was trying to tell them in her room.

The couple walked their way into the familiar hospital lobby of Saint Julian's to the fear of the woman at the counter. She recognized Amelia as the angry French woman who stormed the halls looking for her husband. Thankfully she could see that her husband was alongside her.

Amelia patted her hand on the front desk.

"*Manquer*, we are here to check on a recent arrival." She said abruptly. "A young woman, Sara Ware, *rapidement*." Spencer craned his head over his wife's shoulder while the poor receptionist began flicking through the admission cards.

"Her treatment is likely being covered by Mr Roland Wood?" The Professor suggested.

"Ah! I have it here." She pointed at the card. "Upstairs, to the left, six doors down."

"*Merci beaucoup*." Amelia banged her hand on the table again and took her husband by the wrist to scale the stairway.

Upon reaching the landing, the Coles spotted another familiar face. The same doctor that had treated Spencer when he was here. He was peering into a patient file on a clipboard when he glanced up and noticed the couple.

"Oh, Mr and Mrs Cole." The doctor diverted his full attention to them. "Good to see you again. Nothing amiss in your man's health, I hope. I don't think the hospital needs another lesson in French expletives." He chuckled.

"No, Dr Morrel, I'm in fine enough health," Spencer spoke up while Amelia grinned in amusement at the practitioner's little joke. "We're actually here to check on an acquaintance of ours."

"Sara Ware, admitted for some form of poisoning." Amelia waved her hand while describing their quarry.

"Ware, Ware." Dr Morrel glanced back into his patient chart. "I was just preparing to check on her. It wasn't poisoning though."

"Oh?" They both leaned in simultaneously, eager to hear more.

"No. An above-normal dose of Chloral Hydrate, an unfortunately common ailment we see in young women, but they *usually* come to us much later in the evening." Morrel explained. "Someone was feeling very bold to do this to her in broad daylight, I would say."

"It was done covertly." Amelia showed the label she took off of the bottle in her room.

"*Amelia!*" Spencer scolded her for removing potential evidence from the hostel but she waved him off with a patronizing pat on the shoulder.

"She thought she was taking average nerve pills, but I knew they weren't the normal type." She continued to explain.

"Hm, so you believe someone substituted her pills with a Mickey Finn?" Dr Morrel peered at the label.

"*Oui.* Will we be able to speak to her at any point?" Mrs Cole re-pocketed the slip.

"I'm afraid not. She won't be in any fit state for quite a bit." Morrel shook his head. "She still needs treatment to get that knockout drug flushed safely out of her system, and I want to keep her in a relaxed environment until she's conscious and her condition improves."

The romantic scholars clenched their jaws, both feeling as though they were in a stalemate in a chess match. They offered their skills in finding McClain, but having people on the lookout in no way meant a guarantee of results. They too had a driving need to feel useful, not unlike Essie Cyrus. They never expected just how useful they could possibly be in this case.

"Could we at least be permitted to see her, please?" Spencer asked sincerely with a soft concern in his voice. Dr Morrel paused for a moment, weighing his options as he glanced at them. Finally, he nodded.

"Fine then, but be quick and be quiet." The doctor pointed at them individually, emphasizing the '*quiet*' part as he pointed at Mrs Cole.

The Coles agreed and made their way to the room that they were told Sara would be in. Spencer hoped that the room would be as empty as his room was when he was being treated. Each of the closed rooms had three to four beds for patients to rest while receiving care.

"*Mon amour,* if we can't speak with her, what good is visitation?" Amelia questioned her husband. Spencer dug around in his tight jacket and pulled out a notebook.

"On top of just wanting to be sure she's fine, I want to leave a note for her to contact us or the rest of the Society whenever she feels up to it." He tapped his head confidently. Amelia stroked his cheek.

"*Mon garçon intelligent.*" She cooed as they entered the room...

The couple ceased all movement in shock as they were *not* Sara's only visitors! The room was devoid of other patients but sitting by her bedside was Kent Mc-Clain! The scarred man sprung to his feet and Amelia quickly shut the door, refraining from causing a slam.

"Wait, Mr McClain!" Spencer exclaimed in a whisper. "We know you had nothing to do with this... not directly, anyway." McClain's defensive stance relaxed a bit and he no longer looked like he was about to run.

He stood there, his eyes shifting between the Coles and the door. He was nervous still, but Amelia rolled her eyes and pulled up a chair from the corner of the room, parking it in front of the frightened smith. He nodded silently and sat back down in the chair he was in when they entered and Amelia took a seat opposite him in the one she brought over.

"*Envie de clarifier les choses?*" She finally spoke up. McClain raised his brow and glanced over at Professor Cole.

"She asked if you would care to make things clear." He smiled, placing his hands softly on her shoulders.

"Well," Kent paused. "If you're willing to keep an open mind about it, I was trying to claim my innocence." He gestured his marred hand to the girl in the bed. "I was apologizing for what happened."

"*La fille* is unconscious." Amelia tilted her head.

"Ah, but dear, theories state that comatose patients can hear everything going on around them." Kent gave his hands a gentle clap and pointed at the professor.

"Spot on, mate." He said. "I just wanted her to know it wasn't me *trying* to do this to her." His face contorted into anger. "I shoulda never trusted those damned things! Y'know who said I should give 'em to the girl, don't you?"

"Michael Tilmann." Amelia's face also turned hard.

"Aye. He's pretentious and self-serving, but every now and again he'd say something that'd make me think the man had *some kind* of human feelings." Kent sneered. "All an act to draw ya in! He suggested I give her some nerve medicine he had, so I obliged and brought her the stuff and a water glass!"

"She took them while we were there asking a few questions." Spencer nodded in understanding.

"When I came back and saw her being loaded into an ambulance, I knew full well what happened and who done it. If I was going to have a chance at proving *I* didn't do it on purpose, I had to scarper."

"Running doesn't do much for one's innocence, Mr McClain." Spencer added once more, his wife nodding in agreement.

"Listen, I ain't been in Oxford much, but if the bobbies here are anything like the bigger cities, they don't give someone looking like I do much of the benefit." Kent held up his arms. "They see scars like *these* and just see another thug instead of a worn-out soldier. I got arrested on the street once 'cos there was a bar brawl around the corner and I *looked* like the scrapping type."

"*Je comprends ça, bon homme.* I know just what it is like to be judged on looks." True enough. Amelia Cole has spent a lifetime of judgment as she is a museum owner, its director, a woman, *and* dark-skinned! The final two have earned her patronizing comments and ridicule her entire life and she has thrown it back in every face that dared to do so.

"Yes, I suppose that makes sense." Kent nodded, slightly embarrassed that he had forgotten himself in present company. "Sorry, missus." Amelia waved him off to assure him that she took no offence.

"Well, if it's friendly ears you want, perhaps you should accompany us back to Everjust for the time being." Spencer suggested, patting his wife's shoulder.

"Everjust?"

"The meeting place of our Criminology Society. It is the abode of *Monsieur* Wood and the current lodging of James Mondey." Amelia explained, standing up and holding her hand out to McClain. He took it and stood up with the couple.

Spencer, before they opted to leave, placed the note he wanted to on the bedside table next to Sara. Hopefully, she would wake up soon. The trio opened the room door, watching carefully as they tried to be discreet. Kent and the Coles made their way to the lobby as nonchalantly as possible, but in a busy hospital, people were thankfully too busy to pay them much mind.

Kent willingly climbed in the back of the Coles' car and they all set off to Everjust. Hopefully, there would be some strength in numbers and they would be able to press reason if the Inspector showed up.

Chapter Twelve

We return to Mr Wood, James, and Inspector Daniels at the inn, who were sitting silently in the dining room, mulling over the information they'd each shared. Mr Wood stroked his beard, trying to hide the fact that he was fighting an amused smile at the sheer stupidity of Elsbeth's attempted subversion. He leaned back in his seat, but both men had known him just long enough to understand his mannerisms.

"Wipe that smile off your face, Wood." Daniels teased, still serious but also flaunting his perception skills. Mr Wood rolled his eyes, perturbed that he couldn't fool these fellows.

"Very well, then. I just find it so ridiculous." He sighed, no longer hiding his grin. "That girl certainly needs a stiff lesson in humility."

"Good luck teaching it." said James as he rubbed his eye.

"Oh, I might have something in mind. But for now, our focus should be on nailing down the true murderer." Mr Wood continued to chuckle.

"Well after learning so much about recent events, I'd best call it into the station." Daniels stood up to go once more to the phone. "Hand me your notebook, Boggs, I want to relay this in detail."

"Right-o, sir!" The constable obliged. James also stood up, straightening his vest.

"Say, when you finish with that, I want to call over to Everjust and see how the others are faring. 'Till then, I'm running up to check on the others." James made his way toward the stairs.

"Just check on Tilmann!" Daniels scolded. "I hear any boards or bedsprings from Brush's room and I'll have you!"

"Relax, business before pleasure, it's my creed." James's statement was met with a sarcastic laugh from Mr Wood. "Oh dry up."

"After you, good sir." Mr Wood got the last laugh with that last statement as they could hear the sound of his fine leather shoes clicking up the wooden stairs.

Mr Wood tried to take a moment and meditate, but he'd been still in this seat for far too long. He too stood up and slowly paced the room, taking glances out the window as he listened to Daniels relay the information.

Both Daniels's call and Wood's eavesdropping were interrupted by a loud slamming sound upstairs.

"Damn it to hell!" They could hear James shout loudly in anger. His shoes stomped back into the hallway and the men clambered to the base of the stairs to meet him.

"Mondey, if you tell me what I think you're going to-" Daniels began as James emerged at the top of the stairs.

"Tilmann flew the coop! Room's empty and his window's wide open." He stomped his way down the stairs to meet the men. "And I'll bet *this* is the big reason." In his hand, James held an envelope written '*To Hammer*'. Daniels opened it and looked at the slip inside. Mr Wood looked over the inspector's shoulder to view it himself.

The note read:

To whomever helped the man in the garden along the way, I wish to meet. Come to the GWR Station and I can promise a clean start.

"Someone attempting to help him?" Daniels queried.

"More likely to *use* him. This is my idiot sister's handwriting." James sneered, snatching the letter back and looking over it. "That brat is going to get herself killed!"

"What do you mean '*use*'? What use could a killer possibly be to her?" Boggs finally proved his existence with a decent question.

"Probably to leverage him into another one of her schemes to be a thorn in my side! But we all know what happens to blackmailers in the mystery stories." James egged the thought on and the men all agreed. The Inspector groaned with the realization and whipped his attention toward the door.

"Boggs, the car! As soon as we get there call the station, I want coppers flooding the place!" Daniels ordered as they ran to the front door. James was following in tow, and the Inspector held his hand out to stop him. "Where do you think you're heading?"

"I may hate my family with a burning passion, but I don't wish death on them. If Elsbeth's in danger, I'm going to be there to help *and* I'm going to rub it in her arrogant face!" James's charming and sharp features contorted into the oddest mix of rage and fear.

"If I leave you here, you're just going to pop in in a cab, right?" Daniels groaned. James didn't answer and just stood there with a steadfast expression. "Oh, fine then! Back of the car!" James patted him on the shoulder as he and Boggs ran to the vehicle. Inspector Daniels glared at Mr Wood who shrugged innocently. "Your Criminology Society is an *affliction* to me, are you aware of that?"

Mr Wood smirked as he watched the three pile into the car and speed off with the siren sounding. The large gentleman sat back down, mulling over events.

"What in heaven's name is all the racket?" The old woman entered from her quarters again.

"Not a thing to worry about, Flora. I suspect soon your inn will return to its peaceful former glory." Mr Wood smiled to reassure her, assuming she could even *see* his face. He returned to his thoughts as many things still bothered him about this case. Some of the threads tied together, but the burning question was, what was this all for? An act of sabotage that claimed a man's life, followed by a coverup claiming another. Now a girl was hospitalized and two equally complicit suspects are in the wind.

Similar thoughts were reeling through Essie's mind back at Everjust. Mr Spinner would be far too important to involve himself in such a small blacksmith's contest. Why, then, was he so invested in sabotaging James's event? And how did he even get into Everjust? Mr Wood had some of the best locks put on every outer door.

"Essie!" A pair of fingers snapped in her face. The fingers and voice belonged to Amelia. "Luv, you've been holding onto that water for half an hour."

"Twenty-one minutes and forty-seven seconds. Not quite half an hour." Cecil corrected the small spitfire while glancing at his watch, yet again.

"Cec, I'm about one minute and fifty-two and a quarter seconds from taking that watch and tossing it in the street!" Andrea hissed with an exasperated smile on her face.

"'*A quarter*'?" Cecil chuckled.

"Egads! It laughs!" Andrea chided the butler, causing him to drop his smile as she and Essie giggled at his expense.

The doorbell chimed, affording Cecil the opportunity to leave the overly chummy environment he was being subjected to. He crossed into the foyer and opened the door to the Coles... and Kent McClain!

"Professor. Amelia." Cecil greeted the Coles cordially but gave a cold smile to McClain. "Come in."

The couple led the way, followed by McClain. Amelia scolded Cecil, ordering him to play nice in her native tongue. Kent stopped in front of the butler and gave his arm a pat.

"Sorry about the rough treatment, mate. Self-preservation and all that." He chuckled nervously. Cecil looked at his sleeve and gave a cold smile.

"No worries, *mate*." Cecil hissed. "I'll reciprocate later."

"Eh?"

"Oh, nothing. Off you pop." Cecil shut the door and led the man into the lounge with the others. "Essie, do help me draw the curtains."

"Right, we don't need prying eyes spotting Mr McClain in here." The petite maid trotted over to help Cecil pull the embroidered drapes shut over the wide lounge window. "So where did the Coles find you, anyway?"

"Popped in on me while I was checking in on Ware at the hospital. I hoped she'd hear me enough to know *I* wasn't the one that done it." He caught the others up on events.

"Well, *we've* had some excitement here at Everjust ourselves," Susan spoke up softly. "Someone had Cecil and Essie at gunpoint." The Coles froze in their tracks before attempting to sit down.

"*Quoi!?*" Amelia shrieked. "Are *vous deux* alright!?" Her almost motherly nature took over and she couldn't even keep her primary languages straight.

"We're fine, Amelia, do either of us have holes in our bodies?" Cecil scoffed. "Oh, and I still need to return your handkerchief, Professor." He left the room to retrieve the personal cloth that had been used to bandage Essie's torn-up hands.

"Sorry about *that* too, luv." McClain pointed at Essie's hands. "That came from the fence, yeah?"

"Oh, yes, but it's nothing. I'll be fine." She smiled sweetly, putting Kent more at ease than Cecil did.

"So who was this fellow who tried to shoot you!?" Spencer redirected the conversation back to the previous subject as Cecil returned, handing the slightly red-stained cloth back to him.

"It was Tilmann, wasn't it?" McClain queried.

"No. It was the enigmatic Mr Spinner." Cecil corrected the smith. "The man who we've confirmed purchased the explosives that killed Jefferey Lane, but to what end, we're not sure." He shrugged.

"The executive from Majority Armes?" Spencer was reeling from the extreme load of information that was being poured at their feet. "How does this tie together?"

"When we find Spinner, we'll ask." Andrea crossed her legs confidently. "I've spread the word to keep an eye out for some jobbie matching his description that did my friends a bad turn." She smirked. "I expect we'll be hearing from one of my *many* pals-" Her sentence was cut off by the phone ringing. "Now!" Andrea chimed as she hopped up and took the receiver. "'Ello, 'ello?" Everyone watched with bated breath as Andrea listened to the caller speak. "Thanks a heap, I owe *you* one now. Kisses!" She hung up and clapped her hands.

"He's been spotted?" Essie asked eagerly.

"Headed toward the GWR. Probably trying to scarper." Andrea replied. "So, who stays and who goes?"

"If you're going then I'm going!" Susan jumped to her feet.

"Nothing doing, Miss." Andrea had to hold back any familiar affection she wanted to send toward Susan since they were in '*mixed company*' with McClain here. "You should leave this to us. Besides, McClain here is going to need some company." She had her hands resting reassuringly on Susan's shoulders with a soft smile.

"I insist that you do the same, Essie." Cecil pointed at his small counterpart who looked put off.

"Are we about to rehash this again?" She huffed. "Over the several life-threatening events we've been through, who among us gets hurt the *most*?"

"I get hurt because I'm often protecting *you* against *your* reckless behaviour. The difference is that I'm capable of taking those hits." Cecil took a look at their current audience and gestured for Essie to follow him into the hall. She stood before him with folded arms. "Please, Essie. If anything were to happen to you on my watch, Roland would never forgive me and worst of all, I wouldn't forgive myself either. I'm asking you, *politely* this time, to please stay put for *my* sake."

Essie stared at her uptight superior for some time, but not in a hard angry way. Instead, she was looking at him with a soft expression until a small smile crept up on her face.

"Alright, Cecil. I'll defend the fort. For now." Essie moved her hands behind her back.

They both started to return to the lounge only to see everyone peering around the corner at them. Cecil scowled at the nosy group.

"It was hard to hear you in here." Said Amelia with a snarky grin.

"Are either of you armed or not?" Cecil snapped.

Amelia opened her blazer to show a holstered Walther Model 4 and Andrea pulled a snub-nose pocket revolver out of her handbag. Cecil nodded and went upstairs to retrieve a defensible weapon for himself. Cecil knew that Mr Wood kept an old sidearm from the War in his desk and went to retrieve it.

Mr Blackbird hurried upstairs, skipping steps carefully, and walked in expedient fashion to Mr Wood's personal lodgings. He let himself in and began an immediate search through the drawers of his desk. Upon pulling the pistol from its hiding place Cecil returned to the group so that they could confer on their plan of attack. They opted to take the two visiting vehicles belonging to the Coles and Susan, albeit the latter is solely driven by Andrea.

Cecil hopped into the passenger seat of the sports model alongside Miss Karras and the two of them led the charge toward the railway station. There was no telling what kind of danger they were heading into, but unlike the other times in the past, they were going to be prepared.

The moment the Coles pulled away in their vehicle, Essie closed the door and looked at the pair that remained with her. Kent was as peaceful as could be, but Susan knew that determined look in the maid's eye.

"Essie?" She spoke warily.

"Do either of you know how to drive?" Essie asked with a mischievous smile.

"I do." Kent shrugged. "But didn't you just promise the toff that you'd stay here?"

"I said I'd hold down the fort. A fort is nothing without its commander." Essie smiled again, making her way to the garage.

"Oh god, Essie, this is *not* a good idea! Cecil is going to throw a fit!" Susan tried to be the voice of reason to the best of her ability, but it was for nought.

"Yes, well, as I said the other day, he's always upset about something." Essie chuckled, brushing past Cook who was just returning with groceries.

"Oi, and where are you ducks off to?" Cook cried out. "And who's the roughneck!?"

"No time to explain, Cook! We'll be back for dinner!" Essie called to the perturbed woman.

"I'll just unload these goods myself then, shall I?" Cook rolled her eyes. "Always on the run, this lot... I'm talking to meself."

McClain aided the ladies by hoisting the garage door open while they piled into the Horch. He was nervous about driving around with two women in the car while there was a search being made for him, but he decided it was best to keep the faith. Kent slipped into the driver's seat of the car and peeled out to go and pick up the Society's mastermind.

Chapter Thirteen

Inspector Daniels, James, and Constable Boggs arrived at the station, practically jumping from the car as they made their way hurriedly into the building. The guard saw the men approaching without intent to stop for a ticket and stepped into their path until he saw Inspector Daniels flash a badge from his pocket.

"What's the word, Inspector?" The overeager guard called out, following them like an excited dog.

"A suspect on the run is meeting a person of interest. Have any fine-dressed ladies with a hoity-toity attitude come through? Dark hair, dolled up face?" The Inspector queried.

"One of these trains is bound for London, mate, you just described half of the female passengers." The guard said sheepishly.

"The one we're looking for is a loudmouth Yank like me," James inserted. "But absence my cordial charm."

"A snotty Yank, aye! She was headed for the platform last I saw, complaining about messing her hem the whole way." The guard grumbled.

"Right, then! Boggs, you and the guard spread the word." Daniels ordered. "Nobody in or out of the station, and I don't want a single train going anyplace. I *do not care* if it's late!"

The guard tried, in vain, to argue the point, but it fell on deaf ears as Boggs dragged him away to speak with the other guards and the train conductors.

James and Daniels slipped through the crowd and scanned the platforms. They silently weaved through the masses, who were in such a hurry to wait, but still only saw the faces of unfamiliar people.

"They wouldn't likely meet among the crowds. Too public." James speculated as he turned back to his constabulary companion.

"Surely Elsbeth wouldn't be foolish enough to try blackmailing Tilmann somewhere without witnesses." Daniels scoffed, but the look on James's face was enough to illustrate the answer. "I see... I'm taking the next platform to check the blind spots. You do the same on this end."

"Understood, go!" James agreed.

Daniels rushed to the far end, making his way around to the far platform while James started his dragnet. He hopped up onto a nearby bench, ignoring the confused stares that he was attracting. James looked for any place that could possibly be accessible, wouldn't be covered in filth, and was away from prying eyes. His gaze lingered on a portion of the building that was used for supply storage. It was perfect. No dirty tools, likely no people, and above all nobody would notice a dead body until the perpetrator was long gone.

James jumped down from the bench and slowly made his way over, noticing that the door was slightly ajar. Peeking in, he could just make out a back door adjacent to the main entrance around the side of the building. Best of all, it was hidden just enough by a rack of shelves so nobody would notice him enter. James was going to have to play this smart because he was not armed like everyone else was. He made his way over to the side door and tested the knob, thanking his lucky stars that it was left unlocked.

As James slowly entered the building, he could make out the voices of people talking. He let the door hang open a bit and crouched down to approach the shelf and peek through the small gap of boxes upon it.

"Why would you want to help me?" He recognized the voice of Tilmann.

"Because this whole fiasco shines a pretty terrible light on my brother, James Mondey. I have a vested interest in making him look bad." James could see his sister facing someone who must have been standing just in front of the shelves that James was hiding behind. "I can help you get away scot-free, provided you do me a favour."

"What kind of favour are we talking?" Tilmann asked. Elsbeth held up two tickets for the train.

"These are for the last train of the evening." She said.

"*Last* train! I need out of here *now!* Everybody's closing in on me!"

"Ah ah. First, you'll burn down the rest of the booths at the event at the park. That should ruin what's left of my brother's already tarnished reputation." Elsbeth smirked. "Do that, and I'll get you all the way to America. Fresh new life. Deal?"

"No deal." Said Tilmann in a frighteningly foreboding tone. James adjusted his view to see Tilmann pull a sharp metal file from the back of his trousers. "Give me those tickets, or I'll do you just like that nosey blackguard at the inn." Elsbeth was taken aback, dropping the tickets in fear.

"Y-you wouldn't. I'm a lady!" She exclaimed.

"Right now, you're what stands between me and freedom." Tilmann prepared to charge Miss Mondey, but James thought quicker than his mind ever had without a tipple. He shoved a box of ticket rolls from behind the shelf, knocking the file out of Tilmann's hand! "*Damn!*"

James rounded the shelves and shoulder-checked Tilmann into the wall. He kicked the file across the room and stood in front of his sister.

"James!?" She cried out. "How did- what are you-"

"Shut up!" He shouted over his shoulder in reply. "And you. Get up Tilmann." The pathetic man coughed from having the wind knocked out of him. "On your feet, snake. I want some answers—real ones." The liar held his hands visibly and managed to get up on one knee.

"Please, just let me go. *None* of this was supposed to happen, I'm innocent!" He begged, tears welling in his eyes.

"Oh, so you *didn't* kill Hammond with a knock to the noggin?" James sneered.

"He threatened me! He was blackmailing me, saying he'd tell what I did!" Tilmann screamed out, his voice ringing in the enclosed room.

"The explosion or the cheating?" James folded his arms as Elsbeth crept up by his side while still remaining behind him.

"Take your pick! He'd apparently followed me when I snuck out to hide my supplies under my forge in the night." Tilmann buried his face in his hands. Now it made sense. Hammond lied about when he'd left because he was stalking Tilmann. Nobody heard the latter leave because he had a lighter step than the former! Hammond withheld the information so that he could try and blackmail Tilmann to drop out of the competition!

"And sprinkle the explosive material into Lane's detergent powder, right?" James speculated. The look on Tilmann's face confirmed it. That was why Hammond had a vial. He likely took a sample of the powder himself that night, not knowing what it truly was, as proof to use against the schyster. "And when Jaqueline heard Hammond head out late at night, it was him following *you*."

"It was only supposed to cause a distraction. A small boom to create panic while I do my work!" He cried out again. "You two are rich toffs! You don't know what it's like to work in a thankless position, the same miserable drudgery every day with nothing to look forward to but old age doing the same worthless thing!"

"You don't even make the watch parts, do you? You just put the parts together." Tilmann looked at him with pleading eyes. James huffed. "Believe me," He grabbed his sister's arm roughly. "I'm no stranger to being stuck in unfavourable surroundings!" He pointed at her. "So you lied to enter something you weren't qualified for just to get some prize money?"

"Yes! But it became so much more! When I found out what the *real* prize was, I did what I did to get a position in the Woodland Company! I'd be set for life if I worked under Roland Wood!" James stepped up and grabbed Tilmann by the shoulders of his shirt.

"How could you even know about that?" He growled. "We weren't going to announce the true prize until we named a winner!"

James was startled by the feeling of a sharp object being pointed at his back. He looked over his shoulder to see his sister still standing in place, paralyzed with fear as she stared at whoever had a weapon to his back. He craned his neck a bit more to see a man he didn't recognize. You, the reader, however, would recognize him as Mr Spinner. His devil-may-care smile made James angry, if only because that was normally *his* proclivity.

"*I* told him of the true prize." Spinner guided James to the side, setting Tilmann free from his grip. Spinner was holding the file that Tilmann was about to use on Elsbeth. James returned to stand between her and the men. "I heard you and the bookworm talking about it at the park. I always keep an eye out for important information. When a rival looks to expand their publicity, one must adapt to make the press a pall."

"'*Rival*'?" James smirked back at the two men. "What did he promise you, Tilmann? That he'd help you win and you could inform on Mr Wood's business strategies to him?" Tilmann's silence and Spinner's grin were all the answers James needed.

"A little extra scratch never hurt." Tilmann shrugged.

"Well I hate to break it to you, but Mr Wood did some research. 'Majority Armes'? It doesn't exist." Spinner's smile faded after James let the cat from the bag. Tilmann looked at his false benefactor incredulously.

"What's he talking about, then?" The dishevelled man huffed.

"Don't listen to him, he's just grasping at straws." Spinner wore his grin confidently again.

"He's been right about everything so far. And on top of that, you lied to me. You said that powder would just distract everyone while *I* won the competition!" Tilmann turned on Spinner, grabbing his crooked tie. Spinner, in turn, put the point of the metal file against Timann's neck. He moved his injured shoulder stiffly from the wound he'd suffered back at Everjust.

"Don't get cold feet on me now, friend." Spinner smiled as Tilmann released his tie.

"What's your game, pal?" James reentered the conversation. "Why make Tilmann the scapegoat? Is this really about trying to affect Mr Wood's business?"

"Oh, Mr Mondey, there are so many moving parts in my operation I doubt that you could fathom them." Spinner started to cross the room to reach the main door. "How else can a business grow if bleeding-hearts like Roland Wood own all the manufacturers? I'm told by the higher-ups that causing a press nightmare would make it easier for us to take advantage of his resources while he's putting out the fires. A bit of corporate sleight-of-hand."

"Where I come from, we call them 'hostile takeovers'," said James.

"Call it what you like. It's just business, friend." Spinner backed out of the storage room, keeping his eyes trained on the Mondeys. "And you, Tilmann. If you wish to stick around and be caught that would be fine by me, but you are welcome to join me in escaping."

Tilmann began to follow Mr Spinner but James charged him, tackling him against the wall! He wasn't about to let two criminals go when he had the chance to get at least one. Spinner spun around and started running, leaving Tilmann in the dust.

James struck Tilmann across his jaw, keeping him on the ground.

"Elsbeth! Your bag, give!" He held out his hand. She hesitated.

"This is a Boretti!" Elsbeth clutched her bag. James growled at her with a searing glare and she relented.

Elsbeth reluctantly handed her bag over to James. He used the arm strap to wrap Tilmann's wrists like makeshift cuffs, also tying him to one of the shelf racks. James scrambled to his feet and grabbed Elsbeth by the arm.

"Come with me." He scolded. She tried to protest but James's manhandling made it impossible to complain in a complete sentence. They pushed out into the crowd and James spotted Spinner approaching the station exit. "Damn!" He glanced to the far platform and spotted the Inspector. "Gabe!" He shouted, waving his hand.

Daniels looked around, indicating that he could hear his name until he finally spotted James and Elsbeth. James pointed at the platform entrance. The Inspector immediately tried to make his way back, crying out '*police!*' to clear a path. He surmised that if James was pointing to the station entrance, someone must be trying to escape!

Spinner chuckled to himself as he entered the station building from the platforms. He checked his watch to make sure he was on schedule, but as he looked up he noticed a familiar face entering the front door. Mr Wood's snarky butler!

"There he is!" Cecil shouted. He started running after Spinner, who retreated back to the platforms. A police whistle echoed out from Boggs as Spinner was pursued by the members of the Criminology Society who had just arrived.

Upon chasing the shifty man to the crowded platform it was hard to tell where among the people he was. Andrea knew one way to find him. It was risky and would cause a panic but she raised her pistol and pointed it to the sky, firing off an echoing shot. Everybody on the platform ducked and screamed but there was sure to be one person upright and running away. It worked, but to the group's surprise, Spinner sprung out from nearby and grabbed Andrea's gun, twisting her arm behind her to use her as a shield.

"Hold it, Spinner!" Daniels shouted, but Spinner placed Andrea between them while keeping the gun trained on the Coles and Cecil.

"I pose that statement to you, Inspector." Nobody dared move as Spinner grinned like a scoundrel. "I hope you don't mind accompanying me for a while, though ladies seldom wish to part my company." He said to Andrea.

"Drop dead, you jake." Andrea attempted to bite his arm, but he merely tightened his grip around her neck.

"We'll take a different train, I think." Spinner chuckled as he backed away from the group. "Just stay where I can see the lot of you."

"You won't get away like this, Spinner," Daniels growled as he gave a loose follow, still training his gun on him.

"I wouldn't place money on the wager. Drop the gun." Spinner demanded, shoving Andrea's pistol into her side. Daniels slowly lowered his sidearm to the floor. "Good. Now if you'll excuse us, I've got a withdrawal to make." Spinner continued to back up, the gun pressing into Andrea's ribcage. Spinner tried to pick up the pace, dragging Miss Karras along.

Just as he slipped out of the front door, still being watched by the police and the Society, Mr Wood and the others pulled up to the station. Essie recognized Spinner from a distance and noticed that he was dragging Andrea along. The small maid immediately opened the door, standing up to see over the roof of the Horch!

"Essie!" Mr Wood reached for her.

"Spinner!" She screamed, drawing his attention!

Spinner pointed the gun at the Horch and fired a shot that panged off of the roof. Essie dropped just in time because Mr Wood grabbed her apron and yanked her into the car, covering her.

Spinner stumbled a bit for some reason, giving Andrea the opportunity to pull free of his grip! She stumbled to the side in her heels and took a dive into one of the planters nearby.

"Gabriel!" Cecil slid Mr Wood's gun across the floor and into the Inspector's hand.

From the moment Essie drew Spinner's attention the events played out so fast that it only took a total of eight seconds before another shot made the entire street scramble into a panic. Spinner crumbled to the ground, dropping Andrea's gun on the paved footpath. He was laid out, breathing hoarsely as Daniels knelt down by him.

"Stay with me!" He slapped Spinner's cheek. "I've still got more than a few questions." Spinner wheezed and his gasps grew more shallow.

"Sh-should've stu-uck to... sh-ow b-business..." Spinner smirked one last time before his head dropped back, his eyes wide open.

"Damn! I was sure I only clipped him!" Daniels closed Spinner's eyes and growled as he stood up.

"Don't worry, Gabe," James patted the Inspector's shoulder as they both looked down at the dead man. "I've got a lovely consolation prize for you in the storage area, old Mikey Tilmann."

"Boggs!" Daniels directed the officer to follow up on that. He saluted and ran off with one of the security men to find the storeroom.

Susan came shuffling up to the station to try and help Andrea out of the potted plants. Mr Wood, Essie and McClain came up not far behind. Daniels tipped his hat to the group before doing a double take. His gaze hardened and his jaw clenched.

"Wood? Cyrus?" Daniels began rubbing his eyes.

"Yes, Inspector?" The pair asked in unison.

"Is there a reason that an AWOL suspect that my men have been canvassing for is in your company that *won't* irritate me?" He asked. The large man and small woman looked at each other and shook their heads in the negative. "It's best I not ask, then?" They nodded with cheerful smiles. Daniels sighed heavily and turned back to the station, trying hard not to explode into a stressful rage.

Cecil, on the other hand, began storming up in a frenzy. He began an unintelligible rant about Essie, *once again*, putting herself in danger with that holler. Mr Wood held him back, garnering another series of scoldings toward himself. Now that the case had been handled, *all* of Cecil Blackbird's pent-up frustrations were ready to flood the streets of the entire town! The sound of his shoes clacking filled the area as he stomped around in front of them.

The other members of the Criminology Society watched in apprehensive amusement as Cecil finally lost his collective mind. Spencer and Amelia embraced as they sighed in relief.

"*Au revoir tout le monde.* My husband and I are going to check back in on Miss Ware at St Julian's." Amelia flourished her hand as she and Spencer began walking back to their motorcar.

"Come to think of it," James smirked. "I have a contestant to check in on myself." He turned to his sister and sneered. She looked at him with a mixed expression of abashed animosity as she tried to pull her arm from his grip, at last. He only gripped her arm tighter as she hissed.

"I hope you realize that you've failed your pathetic attempt to please our father. And once he hears what I have to say, he-" James yanked her arm until they were face to face.

"Don't ever set foot in Oxford again. As a matter of fact, for the sake of *all* those in this hemisphere, don't *ever* come to Europe again." James growled in her face. "Take that train and don't you *dare* have the audacity to enter my life again, or I swear that for once in your life, you will have regrets to haunt you until you die as a bitter lonely old hag." Finally, he released her arm and let her go.

As Elsbeth retreated to parts unknown near the station, the others might have questioned why James would allow her to go.

Two reasons stood out as to why they did not ask. One, they all knew that Daniels would be angry about her getting away, but the Mondey Family would likely get her off with less than a slap on the wrist anyway. No amount of time behind bars, in court, or otherwise would change that. Secondly, it was best not to incur any anger from James by broaching the subject any further.

"Well, I think we've had enough excitement for one day." Mr Wood stated.

"Or a lifetime!" Cecil stamped once more.

"Quite. Oh, and Mr McClain?" Mr Wood patted Kent's shoulder. "Best you stick around and go with the good

Inspector. He's a good man, and he knows that you had nothing to do with what happened to Miss Ware intentionally."

"Thanks for that, old man." Kent nodded and sighed in relief as he rubbed his scarred arms.

"By the by, I could really use a man of your ingenuity and moral standpoints." Mr Wood handed Kent one of his business cards. "If you have time when you get back to London, stop by the local branch. I'd be happy to recommend you as a foreman in my manufacturing plants."

"Foreman?" He queried.

"Sure. I don't want a businessman in a suit to take care of my employees. I want a hard-working man with a good sense of morals and knowledge of the job looking after them." Mr Wood patted his shoulder again with his signature smile, making his moustache curl. "I think you fit the bill to a tee."

"*Roland!*" Cecil snapped from the car. "Get in the car or I'm leaving you here!"

"How do you explain him?" Kent asked.

"I like how direct he is. He isn't a sycophant who treats me like some kind of lesser god because I pay him." Mr Wood shrugged. He waved to everybody as he left to get into the back of the car with Essie, likely to listen to more of Cecil's complaints the entire ride home.

Chapter Fourteen

The last two and a half days were a marathon of business with the police, the public, and the press. Mr Wood was on the phone almost nonstop the entire time, covering costs and trying to keep things running smoothly without fail. Meanwhile, James was trying to hold tightly onto the last vestiges of his lofty lifestyle. The previous day, he had to perform a public apology for the string of events that brought his craft exposition to a grinding halt, which many of the booth owners were still grateful for despite the faults that caused the park's fair to be all for nought. Luckily there were no hard feelings thanks to local businesses receiving boons from being allowed to remain open!

James lay on the couch, having drunk two bottles of whiskey and half a bottle of wine. He was going to have the champagne, but Cecil all but beat him over the head for trying to guzzle their finer items. Mr Wood was willing to allow it, but Cecil was on the warpath with *everybody*.

James groaned as he lay in the study. Oftentimes, his inebriation was either to help him think clearer—since, as previously mentioned early in this account, he is one of the only people in history who functions better when soused—or for a celebration, taking part in one of his debaucherous evenings. For the first time *ever*, he was using these drinks to curb his worries. After all, he evicted his sister from Oxford, harmed and threatened her, *and* failed in his instruction to bring some honour to the Mondey name for a change... he was doomed.

"James?" Essie tapped his bare chest with her index finger. She was hoping he was still breathing as he looked like the definition of the term 'dead drunk'. He was sprawled out on the couch with his shirt unbuttoned, only held onto his shoulders by his suspenders. His pants were such a mess that the pleats were indistinguishable from the wrinkles. Lastly, his shiny black hair dangled over his eyes like a mourning veil. "Oh dear. James?" She poked him again.

"Oohhh..." James groaned. "Am I dead?"

"Apparently not, James." Essie stifled a chuckle.

"Ugh... that's a shame." He sighed.

"Well, breakfast will be served soon. More importantly, I'd suggest you take your feet off the couch. Your shoes are still on and if Mr Blackbird sees that, he'll tear your legs off." Essie tried to drag one of his legs to the floor while the other stayed draped over the back of the furniture.

"Too late." Cecil's voice wafted over James in an eerily calm tone. The reason for his reasonable demeanour, however, was due to his focus on rolling the morning paper up. He promptly began to beat James's torso with the newsprint, causing him to fall from the couch with a raised voice!

"*Ah!* I'm up! *I'm up!* Damn it all!" James screamed, trying to surrender.

"Good. Now stop moping about." He took a glance at his fob watch with a raise of his brow.

"Well excuse me for mourning the loss of my one true passion." Cecil rolled his eyes wondering what '*passion*' that could possibly be. "That being squandering my family's ill-gotten gains."

"And I'm sure that indulging in hedonistic vices is only a fringe benefit?" Cecil scoffed as he pulled James up from under his arms. James teetered on his feet for a moment but managed to steady himself.

"Yes, actually." He nodded with a smile.

"Well, James," Essie patted Cecil's arm to calm him while injecting herself into the argument. "I'm sure Mr Wood would be willing to have you in a position where you could continue enjoying your, ehm, *pleasures*." James laughed loudly and hysterically.

"Oh, no he wouldn't!" James sighed with a wry chuckle. "He's a good man and all but he's still a businessman, and hiring my useless ass would be the poorest decision of his entire career. I'm not so sure I'd take it if he *did* offer. I want to ruin the Mondeys, not Mr Wood."

"I appreciate the thought." Mr Wood's voice echoed from the top of the stairs.

The others sauntered into the foyer and peered up at the upper landing to see Mr Wood, who was leaning on the bannister. He was smiling as he stood in a much more casual fit, with his vest unbuttoned, his collar open, and his pants creased heavily behind his knees, all indicating he hadn't been away from his desk the entire time. Essie had been serving Mr Wood's meals to his room, leaving the rest of them lacking his company at the dining room table.

"Do you need more coffee, Mr Wood?" Essie called up.

"Best not, dear. I've had my fill of the stuff." Mr Wood patted his stomach. "Some nice Darjeeling with one of Cook's baked goods would be preferable."

"Not till you've had a proper meal first," Cecil added with his hand held up. "You know how Cook gets when you skip breakfast." Mr Wood laughed and nodded.

"Oh! And Essie, call the others. I believe celebration is in order!" Mr Wood called out.

"Celebration?" She asked as she and James tilted their heads curiously.

"Yes! Haven't you heard? It seems a prominent American socialite helped to solve a heinous crime!" Mr Wood chuckled.

James and Essie both looked at each other before turning around to see Cecil holding out the paper that he used to swat James with earlier. James snatched the print and took a look at the front page. The headline lauded James, specifically, for aiding the police in solving the dreadful pair of murders, plus the attempt of another of the park's contestants. Particular emphasis was put on his drive to save the others and catch the party responsible with no care for protecting his reputation. The article also decried Elsbeth Mondey for her attempts to hinder the investigation. Much of this was credited as sourced by the very reliable Roland Wood!

The inebriated young man practically jumped for joy with boisterous laughter as he read the piece. Essie clapped her hands excitedly, joining his revelry.

"My head is throbbing right now, but this makes it completely worth it!" He spun on his toe like a dancer, holding the newspaper as if it were one of his many short-term lovers before planting a happy kiss on Essie's cheek.

"You're sure that this is enough to convince your family to resume your livelihood?" Cecil asked.

"One thing that the Mondeys are known for is exploiting loopholes. The loophole I've exploited is that they keep to their word by the letter." He smiled. "They cheat and steal every day because they know how to word things just so and keep everything in writing." James reached into his pocket and pulled out the crumpled letter from his family giving their ultimatum to him. "If it got out that they not only reneged on an agreement but invalidated one with their own family, they would lose their precarious sense of honour. No business would want them to handle investments or serve on a board ever again." James laughed maniacly.

"Also, this article talks about the scandal of Miss Elsbeth trying to compromise the investigation." Essie was scanning the article herself. "I'd imagine that despite the hostilities they have towards you, they'll find her much less preferable at the time." James clapped his hands excitedly and threw up a hand victoriously.

"Cec! Crack open a new bottle!"

"No."

"Then grab me a fresh suit so I can go out and splurge on my own!"

"Get it yourself."

Essie swatted Cecil's arm and trotted up the stairs to retrieve a suit for James from the guest room as requested. Mr Wood laughed at the interactions, realizing that he was due for some freshening up himself. He stroked his beard, as several things still circled in his mind about this case. He retreated back to his room to change while mulling things over. As he got dressed, he couldn't help but wonder if anyone else was having the same thoughts as him.

Inspector Daniels, as you've surely guessed, also kept thinking desperately about something. The gunshot he fired that killed Mr Spinner in no way should have been a kill shot. He insisted on having the coroner check for a cause of death. Everyone was insisting that it was an idiotic idea to look for a cause of death in a man who had been shot.

Daniels had been called to the coroner's office to receive their findings. Upon entering, he and Officer Boggs saw Dr Urth the medical examiner sitting at his desk with his glasses precariously balanced on the end of his nose as he looked over his paperwork.

"Ah, Inspector." He removed his glasses and sighed as he stood up. He was neither young nor elderly, with white temples blending into grey hair atop his head. His mouth was framed with clear lines yet his face was deceptively young. "I could have saved you a trip."

"I wanted to be here in person for this." Daniels nodded, peering from beneath the brim of his hat.

"Well to nobody's surprise, Inspector, your man was killed by a gunshot. He had three wounds." Daniels dropped his hand on the desk firmly.

"Three?"

"Yes, all from different weapons." Urth placed his glasses back on and searched for the paper indicating the specifications of the wounds. "According to the reports on the suspect's death, the smaller wound in his shoulder was a graze caused by a small calibre bullet fired from behind. Wound number two was from an old military-issue revolver."

"The one a civilian associate gave me to finish the job." Daniels nodded again.

"Right, yet the true cause of death was from wound number three; A shot from a mid-range hunting rifle straight through one of his lungs. The bullet was wedged into one of his ribs." Urth handed Daniels the paper with the report describing the findings.

"A rifle?"

"Yes, judging by the angle, I'd say that the shot came from the upper floor of a nearby building."

"What does this mean, Inspector?" Boggs asked.

"It means that he had another associate that didn't want him talking." Daniels placed the papers back down on Urth's desk.

"One of the people from Majority Armes?" The officer asked.

"I don't believe so. Mr Roland Wood confirmed the company didn't even exist, at least not yet. I rather suspect that Majority Armes was a front for something else." Daniels sighed, scratching the back of his head as he paced the office. "And finally, on top of that, there are far easier ways to try and grow your business than sabotaging another."

"You think there are more loose ends to this case?" Boggs asked.

"Undoubtedly, but Blofeld was eager to close the case. He'll never reopen it for me to look into." Daniels huffed. "Thanks anyway, Doctor."

Both men left the coroner's office, the ranking of the pair still thinking aloud to himself. Why was a man killed to cover up an overexaggerated method of sabotage? This was like something out of a bad dime novel. The case was interesting, but the outcome was like a parody of some kind... As though it was meant to reflect a story...

"Inspector!" Another officer called out, trotting down the hall.

"What is it?" Daniels and Boggs stopped short to wait for the young man.

"Message for you." He handed Daniels a slip of note paper.

Inspector Daniels read the paper which asked for his presence at Everjust from Miss Essie Cyrus. Daniels was curious about the invitation but decided it would do him well to go as requested.

Mr Wood's mind was no less sound, but his wardrobe was considerably improved. He wore his favourite brown suit to the dining room while he, Cecil, James, Essie and Cook enjoyed their late breakfast.

"Another incredible meal, Cook." He sighed contently as he patted his stomach.

"Don't flatter me, sir, it was only a couple of eggs and ham," replied Cook with a dismissive wave in his direction.

"Simplicity is sometimes the finest of things. I didn't grow up on fancy decadence, you know." Mr Wood smiled warmly. "Oh, Essie? Did you call the others?"

"Yes, Mr Wood! I think that they should all be arriving soon." Essie stood up and began collecting everyone's plates.

"I'm sorry that I won't be back to make lunch for everyone." Cook joined Essie to aid her with carrying the dishes.

"Think nothing of it, dear. Just take care as you visit your niece." Mr Wood requested of the woman.

A screeching sound alerted everyone to the arrival of who could only be Susan and Andrea. Cecil rolled his eyes and left his seat to open the door for the ladies.

"One day the street out there will be painted black from Andrea's driving." He grumbled to himself.

He did his duty and welcomed the ladies, albeit a bit curtly.

"Come in, and keep it below the speed limit as you enter." Cecil snapped.

"Who spit in your gears, Cec?" Andre asked, hands on her hips as she met his attitude with her own.

"I believe he's still a bit hacked off over the events of the past week," Susan whispered into Andrea's ear.

"That's fine then, but why's he being a beast with *us*? We didn't do anything." The un-submissive maid chided.

"You still dragged me along to that back alley explosives merchant, it counts." Cecil held out his hand, directing the couple into the lounge before drawing the curtains to give them privacy from prying eyes.

"Cecil!" Essie's voice carried in from the kitchen. "If you're being rude to our guests I'll be giving you the cold shoulder for the rest of the weekend!"

"And I'll be coming in there to straighten you out!" Came Cook's voice in a much more booming volume.

Cecil merely huffed and crooked his eyebrow, standing stiffly with his hands behind his back. Susan and Andrea giggled to themselves. Cecil narrowed his eyes at them but knew better than to speak up at this point.

"It seems that there's a new head in this house." Susan snickered, prompting the butler to roll his eyes.

The sound of the door knocker resounded in the foyer, allowing Cecil some short relief from the mockery he was receiving. That was doing nothing for his disposition. Opening the door, he was relieved to see Mrs and Professor Cole. This pair took him much more seriously... well, the Professor does, anyway.

"*Bonjour*, Cecil." Amelia led the way in with Spencer close behind.

"Oh, nearly everyone is here!" Essie clapped happily as she crossed the hallway.

"Nearly?" The butler did a quick count in his head. All of the Criminology Society members had arrived by his reckoning.

"Yes, I also invited Inspector Daniels."

"Oh?" Mr Wood left the dining room on his way to the lounge. "I'm quite glad to hear that, Essie. Well done." He patted her on the head and joined the others in the lounge.

The Coles entered the lounge alongside Mr Wood and Amelia noticed the effervescence that James was giving off. He seemed in brighter spirits than he was during their last visit, yesterday.

"You seem to be doing much better, James." Said Amelia.

"I have all the reason to be." He chuckled. "According to our dearest host, Mr Wood, the Mondeys are going to be feasting their eyes on all the good we've done here this past week by tomorrow!" Mr Wood gave a slight bow at the waist.

"You sent them that article in the paper?" Spencer laughed out loud.

"Not exactly." Mr Wood tried to hide his grin, but the curl of his moustache betrayed him. "I gave the story to the local paper in James's hometown, where *everybody* knows the Mondeys." He chuckled. "As James says, by tomorrow they'll be reading *all* about it themselves."

James was rubbing his hands together, laughing like a villain on a radio programme. He was clearly enjoying the fact that his sister was going to be in far bigger trouble than him for once.

"If you were any more excited, I'd be tempted to offer you a cigarette." Andrea stifled her laughter. James leaned over close to her.

"Had one this morning." He said in a whisper.

"I'm aware. I found the butt in the garden." Cecil sighed. James froze, expecting to be swatted again, but the butler just breezed past him, taking a glance through the curtains. "That'll be the Inspector." He removed himself from the room while everyone continued to discuss matters.

Daniels approached the door halfheartedly, not very sure if he would be in his element here. His previous visits were one thing, but he wasn't on the job this time. He was a guest of people he wasn't in the same class as, not by a mile. However, it was relieving that this particular group was one that he was already acquainted with... of course, while he attempted to keep things professional, he was blissfully unaware that many in this group already called him a friend.

"You just plan on standing out there, all pensive?" Cecil asked, tapping Gabriel's shoulder.

"Oh! Mr Blackbird. Sorry about that." Daniels tipped his hat and entered into the familiar foyer. "Ah, by the way," He reached into his coat and handed Cecil the revolver from the other day. It had finally been processed and now that the case was closed, he could return it.

"Good. I wasn't sure how much longer I could hide the fact that I borrowed that." Cecil discreetly slipped the gun into his cutaway coat.

"Thanks all the same. Is Wood in there?" Daniels pointed to the lounge. Cecil nodded as he slipped over to the stairs to return the gun to its drawer.

"Gabriel! You made it! I'd hoped you would." Mr Wood exclaimed followed by warm greetings from the other members of the Criminology Society as well.

"Hello there everyone." He gave a weak wave before giving Mr Wood a signal to meet him in the hall for a moment. Mr Wood obliged and joined the Inspector.

"What's this about?"

"I wanted to talk to you about something that I don't want to alert everyone to." He tried to keep his voice down.

"Ah, one moment then." Mr Wood turned to the archway to the lounge and he pulled out a small gong from the drawer in the hall.

They had originally acquired it for announcing dinner but between Cecil's punctuality and Cook's carrying voice, they never actually used it. Mr Wood had *just* thought of a use for it. He crept up next to the corner of the lounge and gave the gong a whack! The sound of plaintiff screams rang louder than the bronze dish.

Gabriel snickered into his hand while Mr Wood put the gong back in the drawer. He guided the good Inspector further down the hall and around the corner where the extra telephone was.

"Now, what did you want to say?" He asked.

"It's about Spinner. If that was even his real name." Daniels began, thoroughly intriguing Mr Wood further. "First off, none of my investigations turned up anyone by the name of Spinner in any of the industries of armaments or otherwise. Secondly, *my* gunshot was not what killed him?"

Mr Wood's hand froze mid-stroke on his beard.

"What was it then?" He asked with his eyebrows creasing between them.

"A rifle shot fired from somewhere else on the street. I'm inclined to think that there is more happening here than meets the eye." Daniels scratched at his jawline, trying to figure it out.

"Hm. That's odd. I only remember hearing *your* gunshot." Mr Wood pontificated. "Perhaps there was also more to that weapons manufacturer angle than we thought."

"Sir?" Daniels urged for more information.

"There are devices that can be affixed to the end of a firearm to suppress the sound of gunshots. They were being made shortly before the Great War and are quite popular in the States." Mr Wood explained.

"I see! So our gunman likely had one of these suppressors on his rifle, making it nearly impossible to realize what had happened. After all, the only reason I know about this is because I was certain that I hadn't aimed for anything lethal."

"So the gunman was counting on the police just assuming the cause of death to be a bullet and leave it at that." Mr Wood chuckled. "They didn't account for *you*."

"Yes, but unfortunately, Blofeld has proudly declared the case closed. There's not much else I can look into without cutting into my other assignments." Daniels sighed, tugging at the brim of his hat.

"Ah, I understand." Mr Wood nodded with a smirk. "*You* cannot look any further into it. But an independent agent with time on their hands and a vested interest, on the other hand." He chuckled, pointing to himself.

"Exactly!" Daniels snapped his fingers. "All I ask is that you do this privately. You *alone*. I don't need it getting out that this whole Society of yours is poking their noses into things and getting into danger."

"I understand. However, I think you misspoke." Mr Wood smiled.

"Oh?"

"You said this Society of mine. I think you mean '*ours*'." Daniels tilted his head, glancing up at the giant man from under the brim of his hat.

"What are you talking about?" He asked.

"Daniels, you've become as much a member of the Criminology Society as anyone here." Mr Wood patted the Inspector's shoulder. The policeman was speechless for a moment.

"I think not." He replied. "I'm not a wealthy member of society or whatever this is."

"Neither are Cecil, Essie, or Andrea. Money does not determine one's place in this group, a love of mystery does." Daniels frowned.

"That's the thing. I *don't* love mysteries. I work to uncover and end them—to put away criminals who hurt people." Daniels's tone was very sombre. "If you knew the things *I've* done to reach this position, you probably wouldn't find me very moral for your group."

"Ha! I think you would be surprised about what I know about you." Mr Wood flashed a knowing grin at Daniels, just as he did once before. "On top of that, I think you'll find that you aren't the *only* one in the Criminology Society who keeps secrets. Besides, does James Mondey seem like the most moral type of man at first?"

"Well, no, but then he *is* American."

Both of them shared a hearty laugh before Mr Wood put his arm over Gabriel's shoulder and guided the younger member to join the others in the lounge.

Each member greeted Inspector Daniels and they all relaxed with the comfort of each other's company. Daniels was as entertained as everyone else to know the new developments in James's situation. It was good to know that Elbeth Mondey hadn't truly escaped the consequences of her actions.

They all moved on to Susan's latest literary obsession, allowing Daniels to officially be introduced to the true meaning of the Criminology Society.

Epilogue

Another case closed for the Criminology Society. That was rather touch-and-go there for a stretch. All in all, however, I would call my endeavour a complete success. Someday I will have to thank my old friend, James for coming up with the perfect hair-brained scheme for me to insert a suitable diversion. Thanks to that hullabaloo at the park, the police have yet to notice my acquisitions from Lloyd's Bank. Why *would* they when an explosion, claiming a life, rocked the Univerity Parks?

It's incredible to think how easy it is to divert attention. People are incredibly gullible, and crafting a convincing mystery is the only way to keep clever people like my old friends diverted where I want them. A shame that I had to do away with George. He was quite entertaining, but he was also a great risk to my operations. Judging by his rogue behaviour, showing up at Everjust to press intimidation on the Society, he was too much of a wild card to keep in the deck. I suppose that's to be expected when one hires an overconfident actor to play a part. It is a good thing Morton Raan is a good shot, and equally so that I knew where to order sniper's nest since

I predicted the actions of the Criminology Society. But as Amelia might say, *c'est la vie*. And the best part of it all is that I can now manage my funds without sneaking them out of the trust in Mr Wood's care. It may take a considerable amount of time before they catch on to the things I've been up to. I was so certain they would have caught on by now, but thankfully they are all blissfully unaware of the shadowy empire I've begun constructing. I suppose, in the end, the genius of my cover operations is in their simplicity.

Majority Armes;

James Moriarty,

I find it entertaining that they haven't spotted it yet! Just as well, because now I can expand my operations. I may start branching out to London soon. After all, there is only so much space for a criminal empire to build in a small academic community like Oxford.

Dr Zilchrist, however, is starting to become a problem. I think he is catching on to the fact that I am not as '*sick*' as I pretend to be. I think it may be the lack of atrophy in my body. Pretending to be an invalid shouldn't mean I have to *become* one so I tend to take a stroll at night through the ward where the lunatics are held. Who would believe them? But Zilchrist is clever. I'll have to keep a watch on him.

My nurse is late. I hope she isn't getting cold feet about aiding me in my subterfuge. I just got rid of *one* subordinate, I can't be losing more people when my fledgling network is becoming greater by the day! Perhaps I should make a grand but subtle gesture to keep the rest in line. I've managed to gain control over most of Oxford, and I won't let it slip away now. I'm finally fulfilling my dream. Soon, I *will* be the real-life Napoleon of Crime. I *will* be the greatest criminal mind in all of history.

Forgive me a nefarious laugh written in this journal entry,

Ha ha ha!

J.L. Dumire is a growing author building a career in the one thing they love most - entertaining fiction! Born in West Virginia and currently a New Jersey inhabitant, they hope to develop this dream to be able to devote more time to their loved ones while creating suspenseful enjoyment for others. This author has two primary interests in their genres: Urban Fantasy, depicting magic and mythology in a modern setting; and Mysteries, such as their Criminology Society series with twists and turns to keep you guessing who done it until the very end! J.L. Dumire can also be found on YouTube as a member of The Roadrunners gaming channel and on Wattpad as Harlequin-Writer. On the writing community website, they create hobby works such as Detective Dark, an original series about a noir superhero with more to come!